HAVOC

KER DUKEY

HAVOC

ROYAL BASTARDS MC #4
NOVELLA
BY KER DUKEY

ALSO BY

YONDER ORIGINAL

Kings of sin (An Dark MC Series)

Standalone Novels:

Lost

I See You

The Beats in Rift

Devil

Lost Boy

Dark Queen

Kings Of Blood & Money

Exclusive to YONDER

Kings of Sin series.

Empathy Series:

Empathy

Desolate

Vacant – Novella

Deadly – Novella

The Broken Series:

The Broken

The Broken Parts of Us

The Broken Tethers That Bind Us – Novella

The Broken Forever – Novella

The Men by Numbers Series:

Ten

Six

Drawn to You Duet:

Drawn to You

Lines Drawn

Royal Bastard MC Series:

Grim (Newsletter exclusive)

Animal

Rage

Carnage

Co-Written with D. Sidebottom

The Deception Series:

FaCade

Cadence

Beneath Innocence – Novella

The Lilith's Army MC Series:

Taking Avery

Finding Rhiannon

Coming Home TBA

Co-Written with K Webster

The Pretty Little Dolls Series:

Pretty Stolen Dolls

Pretty Lost Dolls

Pretty New Doll

Pretty Broken Dolls

The V Games Series:

Vlad

Ven

Vas

KKinky Reads Collection:

Share Me

Choke Me

Daddy Me

Watch Me

Hurt Me

Play Me

Joint Series

Four Fathers Series:

Blackstone by J.D. Hollyfield

Kingston by Dani René

Pearson by K Webster

Wheeler by Ker Dukey

Four Sons Series:

Nixon by Ker Dukey

Hayden by J.D Hollyfield

Brock by Dani René

Camden by K Webster

The Elite Seven Series:

Lust – Ker Dukey

Pride – J.D. Hollyfield

Wrath – Claire C. Riley

Envy – M.N. Forgy

Gluttony – K Webster

Sloth – Giana Darling

Greed – Ker Dukey & K Webster

ROYAL BASTARDS MC SERIES

FOURTH RUN

Deja Voss: Forbidden Bruises
Darlene Tallman: Brick's House
Nicole James: Keeping the Throne
Shannon Youngblood: Kingdom and Kourt
India R. Adams: parting for Thunder
Jessica Ames: Into the Dark
J.L. Leslie: Worth the Pain
Nicole James: Climbing the Ranks
Elle Boon: Royally Judged
J.L. Leslie: Worth the Trouble
Kristine Dugger: Familiar Taste of Poison
Kathleen Kelly: Creed
K.E. Osborn: Alluring Abyss
Murphy Wallace: Injustice and Absolution
Ker Dukey: Havoc
Dani Rene: A Beautiful Monster

Royal Bastards MC Facebook Group - https://www.facebook.com/groups/royalbastardsmc/
Website- https://www.royalbastardsmc.com/

CLUB CODE

- PROTECT: The club and your brothers come before anything else and must be protected at all costs. CLUB is FAMILY.
- RESPECT: Earn it & Give it. Respect club law. Respect the patch. Respect your brothers. Disrespect a member and there will be hell to pay.
- HONOR: Being patched in is an honor, not a right. Your colors are sacred, not to be left alone, and NEVER let them touch the ground.
- OL' LADIES: Never disrespect a member's or brother's Ol'Lady. PERIOD.
- CHURCH is MANDATORY.
- LOYALTY: Takes precedence over all, including well-being.
- HONESTY: Never LIE, CHEAT, or STEAL from another member or the club.
- TERRITORY: You are to respect your brother's property and follow their Chapter's club rules.
- TRUST: Years to earn it...seconds to lose it.
- NEVER RIDE OFF: Brothers do not abandon their family.

AUTHOR NOTE

This is a Royal Bastards **Novella**
following Lily's story
Read with caution.
Contains scenes that may cause triggers from the start.

CHAPTER
ONE

PAST.

LILY

Fifteen years old...

"Drink up, Lily."

No.

"I don't want to." My hand tightens around the glass, my knuckles turning white. The snowy crushed tablets swirl in the water, settling at the bottom of the glass. The air condenses, suffocating me. Yellow flowers on the wallpaper wilt before my eyes. The old wooden chair digs into my thighs, my foot tapping manically beneath the table. The dull, outdated kitchen makes me want to vomit.

I hate it here.

The words don't make it past my lips, fear holding

them hostage. The last time I spoke those words, I couldn't walk for a week. Grandma's paddle hangs on the wall like a medal, mocking me from across the room.

"It's better for you if you drink it," Grandma tells me. I know she's right. It will silence the voices. Block out the pain inflicted in the dark. Drown out the betrayal.

No.

"Drink it." She glowers, pushing my head toward the glass, her jagged nails scraping against my scalp. Tears burn the corners of my eyes. My stomach growls, wanting to eat the small portion of food before me. Ever since I hit fourteen and my boobs became noticeable, Grandma began limiting my meals, like that was the reason I was changing into a woman. Now, my bones protrude from the skin. I can't stand to look at myself in the mirror.

"Drink, Lily." Her voice is sharp, stabbing into me. Wounding.

Please don't make me.

To drink this poison makes me complicit in some way.

"Drink or you won't see your brother this weekend."

A pit opens in my chest. I don't want to see Jameson. What if he sees the dirt on my skin, the sin, the disgusting stains that litter my soul?

"No!" I shout, throwing the glass across the kitchen.

It slams against the fridge and shatters, making a loud sound that shocks us both. My heart pounds behind my ribcage. Panic ravages my thoughts. My bladder threatens to empty on the kitchen chair.

"You ungrateful little devil child. Get to your room now," she scorns snatching my plate away.

I need that food.

My hands shoot out to stop her, but it's too late. My fingers thud against the tablecloth, the plate out of reach.

"Room. Now." She jabs a finger, and my breath hitches. I look at the door but don't move. Gentle tremors shake my hands.

Kill her, Lily.

The thought creeps in from the shadows of my mind, rolling in like a tide to wash all the fear away, all the pain she's caused me.

"What's going on?" Grandpa's raspy voice calls from the basement. My stomach twists. Nerves chew beneath the skin, trying to get out.

"Do you want me to tell him to come up here?" she asks, narrowing her small, crinkly blue eyes at me.

My voice catches in my throat. I want to scream, *Why!* Instead, I say, "No," shaking my head vehemently.

Pushing the chair back from the table, I stand and hurry down the hall, closing the door to my room as soon as I enter. Slumping back against it, tears fall down my cheeks as the lock clicks into place.

This room is full of furniture, dolls, soft toys, but I'm hollow. Candy cotton pink walls and embroidery drapes left untouched from when my mother slept inside these four walls. They do nothing to offer comfort. Mama's six feet under, rotting in a casket.

The world was too much for her.

I was too much.

How could she leave me to this fate?

I don't know how much time passes, but I know something bad is coming. The wait is almost too much to bear.

Sitting in the corner of my room, I grip a soft teddy bear until pain aches my fingertips. The chime of the doorbell signals the visitor who haunts my nightmares.

Please go away.

Please go away.

Mumbled voices followed by footfalls stopping outside my room blast like a siren in my head.

The latch clicks. The handle drops, and so does my stomach.

No. Go away.

Panic seizes my joints. I can't move.

The door creaks open, the imposing figure filling the space. "Hello, little love."

Sickness roils my stomach.

"I want the drink," I plead, the words clawing up my throat.

The man steps into the room, licking his lips. "Remember, no visible bruises," Grandpa tells him, he and Grandma standing behind the man looking in at me.

What about the internal ones? The mental ones? *Why don't you love me?*

"Grandma, I want the drink," I plead.

"You should have thought about that." Her evil face twists.

The man reaches for his belt as the door slams and the lock engages. "Be a good girl. I'm not going to hurt you," he spills his lies, taking off his jacket and hanging it on a hook on the door.

I want to die too.

Mama went to heaven and left me in hell.

The man pulls off his collar and places it on my doll house. The devil disguised as a man of god.

"On the bed, Lily. Be a good girl."

One day, I'm going to kill them all.

Heaven be damned.

CHAPTER
TWO

PRESENT

LILY

Twenty years old...

"She's fucking crazy," the little wimp cries out, nursing his hand against his chest, red liquid dripping to the floor at his feet.

"Why the fuck did you stab him?" Rage exhales, sick of my shit. He's sitting at a table in the main room of the clubhouse with our prez and two guys I don't recognize. My gaze is drawn to the one fidgeting with a lighter, twirling it in his hand, glacier blue eyes focused on the action.

"He grabbed my ass," I snap, justified.

"She was bending down, waving it in my face,"

Milk whines. Only in our chapter a month and he's already outstayed his welcome.

"I was tying my fucking boot, you grubby little shmuck." I should have stabbed his tongue, then I wouldn't be standing here getting tattled on like some pre-school bullshit.

"So, if you stabbed him, why the hell is your ass cheek bleeding?" Rage points to my ass. Frowning, I look to see the small gash in my jean shorts oozing blood down the pocket. Fuck. I love these shorts.

"His hand was on my ass when I stabbed it." I shrug.

"Wait—" Animal shakes his head, "—you stabbed your own ass to punish, Milk?"

"I don't like being groped by an inbred freak. I reacted, my ass be damned." In reality, I'd reacted without thinking at all. The anger took over, and the next thing I knew, Milk was wailing like a bitch and my ass stung.

"I ain't inbred, you crazy fucking bitch." I shift my foot in his direction, and he flinches. Pussy.

"Enough." Animal slams his palm down on the table, making it rattle. "Milk, have Doc stitch you up. Lily, for fuck's sake, stop stabbing brothers." *It's only been three.* They all deserved it.

"Is that it? She tried to kill me!" Milk belts out.

"If I wanted to kill you, you'd have a hole in your head, not your hand, dumbass." How this waste of leather ever earned his patch, I'll never know. I roll my eyes and cross my arms, my gaze landing on the new guys again. The lighter twirler is stone-faced, his eyes flitting between Milk and me and my ass, his fist tightening around the lighter. The other one grins like we know each other and share a joke.

Leaning into my space, Milk hisses, "You better watch your back." I fist my hands, itching under my skin to maim him.

"You had to go and do it, didn't you?" Rage groans, rubbing his hands down his face.

A shadow bleeds over Milk's body, heavy-footed boots stopping behind him. "Tell me I didn't hear you threaten my baby sister?" Jameson towers over Milk, dwarfing him.

The color drains from Milk's face. If I weren't royally pissed off, it would be funny. Jameson places a bottle of whiskey on the table, juggling five glasses between his fingers.

Turning, Milk holds up his hand. "She stabbed me."

"You're lucky to still have the hand," Jameson warns him.

"Why do they call you Milk?" the grinner asks, cutting through the atmosphere.

"Because he sucked on his mama's tits until he was a teen." I scrunch my nose.

"I was nine," he defends pathetically, and I almost gag.

"Still fucking gross," Rage points out. A smile curls my lips.

"Can you go and get yourselves cleaned up? You're making a fucking mess." Animal gestures to the small puddle at Milk's feet. My blood has dripped down my leg and filled the back of my boot.

"Monroe is out back with Drew. Have her stitch you up." Jameson jerks his head at me.

"Thanks. I will," Milk grumbles and goes to leave.

"Not you, pervert," Jameson sneers, grabbing his shoulder, halting his steps. "I was talking to Lily."

"Well, who's going to fix me?" Milk looks between Jameson and Animal.

"A therapist?" the grinner pipes up, making himself and Rage chuckle.

"Who the fuck are you again?" Milk asks him. Animal straightens his back and leans forward, steepling his fingers.

"They're my guests. Now, fuck off before I give you a real wound to cry about."

Mumbling under his breath, Milk shuffles away, disappearing out the back exit.

My gaze shifts to the lighter player, his eyes burning into the side of my face. Bold of him to stay blatantly focused on me.

What the hell are you staring at?

The retort is on the tip of my tongue, but it gets clogged in my throat. He seems familiar to me, gravity tugging me toward him. *Do I know you?* It's stupid, that's a face you wouldn't forget. The hairs raise on my arms, energy cackling through my veins, those eyes as clear as the Mediterranean ocean. I want to get ship-wrecked in them.

"Hey," the grinner says, drawing my attention to him. "I agree. Milk deserved it."

"No arguments here." Jameson fills the glasses with liquor.

"Don't encourage her," Animal groans, knocking back his drink in one gulp.

"I'm Leo. This is my brother, Zane. We call him Chaos."

"Lily." I lift my chin, trying really hard not to look at his brother. *Chaos.*

"We call her Lilith, the she-demon." Rage chuckles under his breath, grunting when Jameson boots him in the shin.

"Dick." I scowl, giving him the one-finger solute.

"Enough with the distractions. Lily, go get yourself cleaned up. We have business," Animal dismisses me. I allow myself one last look at Zane, my stomach dipping when his eyes clash with mine. Brown hair pulled back into a low ponytail. A jagged scar cutting through his right brow. Sharply defined cheekbones. Full, fat lips. Tattoos clawing up his neck from the collar of his shirt.

He fits in here. I hope that's what they're discussing.

I like a little chaos.

CHAPTER
THREE

ZANE/CHAOS

"You have your hands full with that one." My brother chuckles, our gazes fixed on Lily as she walks toward the bar and orders a drink, angling her body so she can hear our conversation.

My dick twitches. I admire a badass woman who can take care of herself. Men like Milk only see Pussy when they're around women. He wouldn't have the first clue what to do with someone like her.

He won't let it drop that she stabbed him either. Lily embarrassed him, and one way or another, he'll make her pay for it.

"You have no fucking idea." Jameson guffaws, looking over his shoulder at her and rolling his eyes. "I said go get stitched up," he growls.

"You're not the boss of me. I'll go when I'm ready," she retorts, and Rage's body jerks from a restrained laugh. There's a blood streak from her ass to her boot.

"So, what can I do you for?" Animal asks, clearing his throat, forcing our attention on him.

"Can't we just stop by for a drink?" My brother holds up his glass. We've known Animal for some time now. He was keen to recruit us for his club, but my brother is unstable. Trouble is all he can offer the Royal Bastards. I love him, but he's a liability. Sooner or later, they'll realize that and be forced to do something about it.

"Absolutely, but you asked me to be here for a reason, so here I am. Don't waste my time." Animal grinds his jaw. A grin tugs up the corner of my mouth. I like a no-bullshit approach.

"Straight to business then." My brother shuffles in his seat, his chirpy attitude gone. "I know you have connections with Ronaldo Rossa. He took something of importance from me, and we intend to take it back." He says "we"—he means "me."

"Ronaldo deals in imports, alcohol and flesh—what the hell could he have taken?" Rage raises a brow.

The table falls quiet, and Animal blows out a frustrated breath, rubbing a hand across his jaw. "A woman?"

He's right. My brother has been through more women than Jack the Ripper. He claims this one is different. Who the hell am I to tell him she's not? I've never been in love. I don't see the appeal of tying my emotions to another person. It's only ever cost me.

"She's a dancer at his club and started hiding her tips." Ronaldo is a piece of shit. His dancers have to split their tips with him fifty-fifty. Rumor has it, he forces sex work in an underground club from some of the favored girls. Kelly is a popular dancer and didn't come home two nights ago.

"You think he found out and did something to her?" Jameson asks, leaning forward, placing his hands on the table.

"We think he has her working the members-only area," I say. Lily's movements catch in my peripheral, drawing my gaze. She's closer to the table, lurking in the middle of the room, her brow arched, big brown doe eyes bouncing between me and my brother.

"What exactly is it you're asking?" Rage pours more liquor into the glasses and knocks back his fill.

"If we'll catch any blowback from the Bastards if we make a move on Ronaldo." Leo taps his finger against the glass, looking around the club his attention snagging on a group of brothers playing pool pretending not to be watching our interaction.

"Ronaldo doesn't need us to back him up. He's Arlo Aire's cousin. No one's stupid enough to make a move against him."

"I just want my woman back."

"How do you know she's not there by choice?"

Jameson asks. His size dwarfs the table and could put anyone on edge.

"She's not a whore. Dancing is all she was willing to do."

"We don't plan on making a scene or an enemy. I'm going to go in and get her out. No harm, no foul. Then she and my brother will disappear until they forget about her."

"You're going in on your own?" Jameson's eyes travel over my form, his lips pulling down in a frown. What he doesn't know? Alone is how I prefer to work. Quiet, officiant, and deadly—if need be. It's only when shit turns bad that the chaos comes into play.

"Unless you're willing to spare a couple brothers to help?" Leo shrugs his shoulders, letting out a harsh laugh, his nerves rattling his vocal cords. My brother isn't like me. Our old man beat him constantly growing up, and he witnessed so much horrendous shit happen to our mom, it shaped him into this wary, on edge, frightened human being.

"You know we can't be involved in any of this. This conversation never even happened," Rage informs him.

"We do a lot of business with the Aires. Ronaldo is off limits," Animal adds.

"What conversation?" I stand and pocket my lighter.

"This is a suicide mission." Animal tells me, his jaw ticking. He doesn't think I should do this for my brother. But what kind of man would I be to leave a woman in a place like that knowing she doesn't want to be there?

"It was good seeing you," I turn to leave, pausing for just a moment to look at Lily one more time.

CHAPTER
FOUR

LILY

I pull open the large wooden door and step inside the church, my stomach twisting. Fists squeeze my internal organs until the air in my lungs seizes. My legs shake with the effort to keep me upright. I've been here so many times, always staring at the building from my car, trying to build up the courage to walk inside. Today, I found it.

My gun is loaded and tucked into the back of my jeans. The blade I keep strapped to my ankle is sharp and ready to bleed this place of evil.

Decorative windows and tall ceilings offer a peaceful illusion. A giant cross hangs behind a podium at the back of the room, dominating the space. A mix of musty furniture and candle wax surrounds me. The rows of wooden bench seats are faded from all the god-fearing asses planted in them every week, praying with a man whose soul is darker than the bowels of hell.

My feet carry me down the center aisle toward an open casket surrounded by flowers. My heart pounds against my ribcage, in sync with the throbbing of the stitches in my ass cheek. As I get closer, I see a body inside. A young woman. Hollowed cheeks painted in the mortician's makeup, the rouge overly red for such a young girl.

What happened to you?

Her black dress stands stark against the white satin lining. Her arms are folded to rest on her stomach, almost in prayer.

"Are you a relative? The service doesn't start for another hour."

His voice crashes into me like a sledgehammer, bashing down the walls I'd built up. Sirens blast through my brain. Everything I've fought to overcome tumbles to ash.

"Get on the bed, Lily."

Why did I think I could do this?

Shoving my trembling hands into the pockets of my jacket, I shake my head. My hair bounces around my face, hiding me from view.

"How did you know her?" He steps closer, and acid burns in my stomach. His darkness creeps over me, draping me in dirt until it fills every pore, invading every hole, turning my bones to cement. I can't move. I'm back in that room, cowering beneath his torment.

"Get on the bed, Lily."

No!

I got out.

I got out.

"No!" I scream as his hand lands on my shoulder. Spinning around, I barge past him and race for the door, tears cascading down my cheeks, blurring my vision. Pushing out the door, I grip the railing of the stairs and fold into myself, my legs turning to jelly. I gasp, dragging gulps of air into my lungs, my fists clenched.

He has no power over you.

It's a lie.

The door behind me opens, and like a frightened rabbit, I jump up and dart across the street. Getting into my car, I drive away without looking back.

I'm not strong enough.

I have to be.

I pull into Kirby's Bar, swinging my car into the first parking spot I come to. Shoving my gun into the glove compartment and slamming my hands on the wheel, a strangled scream retches from the deepest parts of me.

Fuck. Fuck. Fuck.

I swipe the tears from my eyes and take a deep breath, frowning when I recognize the people coming from the bar and walking past my car.

Chaos.

Without thought, I jump from the car, the gravel crunching under my boots.

"Hey! Wait up!" I call out as they make their way across the lot to their bikes. The scent of summer rain clings to the air and dampens the roads. Rays of sunshine soak through a break in the clouds, warming my skin.

A smirk tugs up Leo's lips when he sees me approaching them. Chaos stands with his legs slightly parted, his hands clasped, dangling below his waist-band, head tilted, studying me.

"Twice in one day, lucky us." Leo beams. "What can we do for you?"

I'm focused on his brother when I say, "I'll help you."

Leo's deep chuckle hums through the air, washing over me. "With what?"

"Getting the girl back."

Leo shakes his head, looking around to make sure we're still alone. "I don't think your brother would like that."

"Why?" Chaos interrupts, his brow pinched. "Why do you want to help?"

I step closer, until we're almost boot to boot, nerves bouncing around inside my stomach. My head is fuzzy, my eyes swollen and burning. "Because I want you to help me with something in exchange."

The wind picks up a scattering of leaves, swirling them around our feet. The trees looming over the parking lot sway, the heavy branches hanging like gallows.

"Zane, come on. Animal won't like this either."

"I don't see anyone else lining up to help you." A lump forms like a brick in my throat. Desperation seeps from my pores.

"What makes you think I need help?" Serenity gleams from Zane's ocean-blue eyes. I want to bathe in them, soak up every part of him, calm the turmoil ripping me apart.

"Because, if you really thought you could get in and out undetected, you wouldn't have come to the club earlier asking if the brothers would come for you if shit turned bad."

"Animal's a friend. We came out of respect."

"Let's help each other."

"Sweetheart, I don't think you'll be much help." Leo frowns, running his gaze down my body.

"My name is Lily—and you have no idea what I'm capable of." I narrow my eyes.

Leo holds his hands up in surrender then swings his leg over his bike and pulls on his helmet.

"What is it you need help with?" Zane asks, licking his lips. My stomach dips, but it's definitely for other reasons.

"Some trash needs taking out." I drop my gaze to the knife sheafed at my ankle and lift my pant leg.

He jerks his chin to my ass. "Milk?"

Rolling my eyes, I shake my head. "He was barely

worth the effort of a hand-wound. Someone else. And I don't just want to harm them, I want them dead," I say in a hushed murmur, my teeth gritting.

"That is a dangerous favor to ask of someone, Lily—especially someone you don't know." He leans in close, whispering into my ear. "What makes you think I'm a killer?" He breathes out against my cheek, sending a wave of goosebumps across my skin.

I place a hand on his chest and take a chance. "Let's just say I recognize a kindred spirit." As crazy as it sounds, it's the truth. I'm a balloon tethered to a string, and he's pulling me toward him. Part of me knows it's reckless, but I need this. His heartbeat thunders beneath my palm. He's not unaffected by me.

"Get on." He nods to his bike before sweeping his leg over and waiting for me. I climb on behind him, clutching his waist, and pin my thighs to his. Adrenaline spikes through my veins as I glance back at my car. Jameson is going to bitch me out for disappearing, but I'm grown, and I need to do this.

The engine roars to life, vibrating beneath me, drawing a smile to my lips.

I need to face my demons and destroy them.

CHAPTER
FIVE

ZANE/CHAOS

Her thighs squeeze against mine, and a rush of hunger claws through my body. I've never put a woman on the back of my bike. I'm one of those assholes who fucks a willing woman at whichever bar I'm visiting that night, never even getting a name.

This is just me giving Lily a ride to Leo's, but there's something I like about it. The warmth of her body covering mine…

I get the feeling she's hell fire and I'll be begging her to burn my soul.

Pulling into the drive, I park my bike next to the truck and wait for her to climb off.

The heat of her body leaves mine, and she stands there awkwardly, brushing her hair with her fingers.

"How's your ass?" Leo asks, walking past her up the steps to the front door.

"Tender." She smiles tightly and looks at me. "It was worth it. Milk is too handsy—and not just with me."

Climbing from my bike, my eyes drop to her ass encased in a pair of skin-tight jeans. "Sacrifice is necessary sometimes." I gesture to the house. "Come on."

Apprehension pinches her features. "We don't bite." I hold my hand out to her, and she lets out a breath, taking it. Once we reach the top step, she drops my hand and shoves hers into her jacket.

"Is it just you two who live here?" she asks as we enter the house. It's dull inside, the place untouched from when mom decorated it over twenty years ago. Leo throws himself on the old brown couch, the foam from inside showing through slits in the fabric. He rests his foot on the old, beaten-down coffee table covered in scratch marks and cup rings. Flower patterned carpet runs through the entire house, the pile worn down to almost nothing. It's a shit hole.

"This is Leo's place." I fucking hate being in this tomb.

"You don't live here?" She moves deeper into the house, cautious, a shiver racking her body.

"I stay here when he needs me to," I inform her. It's usually after he breaks up with whichever woman has become sick of his shit. My brother is bipolar and takes weeks off his meds, spiraling his moods. Mix that with his childhood trauma, night terrors, and paranoia, and you're left with someone highly dangerous to you and himself.

"I'm ordering pizza. Pepperoni good with you, Lily?" Leo calls out.

"Fine. Thanks." She folds her arms, trying not to touch anything. I should have taken her back to my place.

"Let's go in the other room and talk." I lead her through the kitchen into the dining room. She takes a seat at the table, wincing as she does. The table is the only thing Leo's bought for this house, barring his flat screen tv.

The floorboards above us creak, drawing Lily's attention. "Is there someone else here?"

"No. It's an old house." I shrug. She probably wouldn't believe me if I told her the place is haunted.

A nervous laugh trickles from her lips like music. "Okay."

"So, tell me about this person you want taken care of and why you haven't dealt with it yourself or had your brother deal with it?"

Her shoulders stiffen, and something dark shadows her eyes.

"There are some things you can't tell your brother. I have a brother-in-law I've thought about talking to. He would do this for me. But things would never be able to stay how they are now if I told him."

"You don't want them to see you differently," I surmise.

"Exactly."

"You'd be surprised what a brother is willing to do for their sibling." I've killed for mine.

"I have no doubt Jameson would burn the world down for me if he thought it would keep me safe, but he can never know the ways I suffered every time he sent me home after weekends I'd spend with him. He wouldn't survive it."

A tear leaks to her cheek, and she angrily swats it away with the back of her hand. Someone hurt this girl's soul deep. I know what that feels like.

"I'll help you." Her mouth pops open, forming the perfect O, her thick lips dusted in pale lipstick.

"You haven't even asked who it is or what he did." She places a hand on the table, rubbing a small smudge with the pad of her finger.

"I don't need to."

I reach across the table to place my hand on hers, but she flinches away, twisting her lips, "I don't want pity," she snipes.

"That's not what I'm offering." I draw back, leaning against the back of my chair to give her some space.

"Then what is it you're offering?"

I shrug, giving her words back to her. "A kindred spirit who recognizes your pain and is offering to help in seeking vengeance."

A silent pause hangs between us, just our breathing and the faint buzz of the TV coming from the living room.

"Why do they call you Chaos?" she asks, finally breaking the silence, her big brown eyes steady on mine.

"Because it's what I cause when anyone crosses me." I wink at her and waggle my brows.

A beautiful smile takes over her whole face, and I want to capture a picture of it to look at whenever shit gets heavy.

"So, we have a deal—I'll help you after you help me?" She holds her hand out for me to shake.

Slapping my palm against hers, I grip her hand and jerk it in a shake. "Deal."

CHAPTER
SIX

LILY

This place reminds me of my grandparents'. Darkness clings to the atmosphere, clogging my throat. I need to get out.

"Pizza's here," Leo calls out as the front door slams, vibrating the foundation.

Leo appears in the doorway holding two pizza boxes, half a slice stuffed in his mouth. "What's the verdict?" he asks around the food. Standing, I take the boxes from him and place them on the table.

"I'm going to help bring your woman home." I flip the lid and take a slice. The aroma clings to my taste-buds, making my mouth water. Since getting free from my grandparents, I never miss the opportunity to eat when it's presented, and the weight went on quick. My ass, chest, and hips are much fuller than they used to be, but my legs are still twigs.

"You sure about this?" Leo asks Zane, moving around him to take a seat on the opposite side.

"We could use the help."

"What's the plan?"

Getting to his feet, Zane says, "I'm going to take Lily back to her car."

"Wait—" Leo holds out his hands, "—that's it?"

"I told you I'd deal with it if you let me do it my way," Zane informs him.

"I am letting you do it your way, but I still want to know what the plan is."

"You will know when you need to."

Tension creeps through the air.

Picking up the pizza box, Leo launches it across the room. It crashes against the wall, sauce and toppings flying everywhere. My heart rate accelerates. I don't even realize I've gotten to my feet and put my back to the corner of the wall, hands outstretched in defense.

"It's fine, Lily," Zane assures me. I grit my teeth, mad the run-in today rattled me so badly. An outburst like Leo's wouldn't usually faze me, but I'm on edge, and it was so unexpected.

"You need to calm the fuck down and think for a second," Zane warns his brother.

"I'm sorry, okay? Fuck knows what she's being made to do down there while I'm sitting here eating pizza." Leo paces.

"We'll get her out, but we have to play smart. You're no good to her dead—and that's what we'll both be if we fuck this up."

"I know." Leo rubs his hands down his face and turns to me. "I'm sorry, Lily. You don't need to fear me."

"I don't fear anyone." Lies. "I'll be outside," I inform Zane, pushing out of the room.

Fresh air bathes over my skin as I race down the porch steps. The orange and pink rays of the setting sun illuminate the sky, casting a warm hue through the trees.

I probably should have probed Jameson for more on these brothers before confiding in Zane and offering to help them, but this is the only way I'm ever going to rid of my demons. Ezekiel would do this for me, but he wouldn't keep secrets from my sister, Ruby, and she would tell Jameson.

I can't do that to them. Infecting them with that knowledge is cruel. It's bad enough I have to live with it.

"You okay?" Zane asks, coming down the steps.

"Fine. What was that about?" I wave a hand back toward the house.

"He can be unpredictable, that's why he can't help me with this."

"Do I get to know the plan?" I ask, rubbing my hands down my arms to ward off the chill dusk brings.

"I thought we could go over your job first, then go

to the club tomorrow and see what we're dealing with." He gestures to the truck. "Hop in. I'll take you back to your car. We can talk on the way."

Opening the truck door, I heave myself inside, the stitches pulling a little. The drapes twitch upstairs movement shadowing the window. "Will he be okay with you gone?" I bite my lip, an unsettled pit opening in my stomach.

"He handled being on his own for a few years, I think he'll be okay for a few hours."

"Where were you in those years?" I swivel my head to look at him. The pit widens when he frowns, backing the truck out of the driveway.

"Doing some time in juvie and a small stint in prison."

"Do I want to know what for?" I shift, pulling the seatbelt into place. Digging into his pocket, he pulls out his lighter and flicks it open and closed against his leg.

"I killed our dad." He says it so casually, it takes a moment for the words to register. Wild horses gallop in my chest. My mouth goes dry. "He deserved it and more, trust me," he adds.

"And you were caught?" I ask, curious.

He looks over at me, amusement lighting his eyes and tugging up his lips. "That's your question?"

I shrug. "Yeah."

Chuckling, he says, "I was young, and it was in front of my mom. She called the police."

"She didn't try to stop you from killing him?"

"There was nothing to stop. He came in drunk while we were carving pumpkins for the town contest. Leo had been looking forward to it so much, and Mom actually bought the pumpkins that year." He shakes his head, a war raging on his face. "Dad came home early. I remember the burn of his breath on my skin." He grips the wheel harder, making it creak under the stress. "Went ballistic over the mess and started wailing on Mom. The bruises from her last beating had barely been healed."

My breath hitches, each word from his mouth a physical blow. Walking on eggshells, not knowing what will set the person off, enduring the beatings, the betrayal, the pain, not understanding how someone who's supposed to love you can be so cruel…

I know that nightmare all too well.

"Then he turned on Leo. I never understood his hatred toward him until I got older." He looks at me, lines marring his forehead and crinkling around his squinted eyes. "It was because he was different. He struck him, and Leo dropped, out cold. I thought he was dead."

I reach out to steady the lighter lid clicking open and closed. Curling my fingers around his hand, I squeeze. His eyes drop to our contact, his breathing heavy. Slowing the truck, he pulls into Kirby's. The bar lights dance over the hood in flashing blue.

"What happened next?" I ask, my tone soft.

Inhaling, he squeezes my hand back. "I took the

knife we were using for carving, walked over the top of the table, and plunged it into his chest. One stab. The blade went in on an angle, straight through his ribcage into his heart."

"You were protecting your family." My head bobs up and down, conviction lacing my tone.

"My mother didn't see it that way."

"Fuck her. Why did the police press charges, how could a judge convict? You were protecting yourself and defending your mom and brother."

"I was thirteen. I only got a couple years in juvie. I'd do a hundred years if it meant not watching my brother get beat on. Leo's older than me. He always took the brunt of my dad's wrath after Mom."

"Did your mom ever try to leave?"

"Fuck no. She loved the son of a bitch and always made excuses for him."

"Where is she now?"

"Lost her shit. She's in and out of hospitals and rehabs."

"You said you served prison time?"

"Caught that?" He smirks. "I did three years for carrying a firearm without a licence."

"Harsh." I fidget, thinking of the gun in the glove box of my car. No license for me either.

"Now that I've spilled my dirt, you want to spill yours?"

Giggles and raised voices carry from the bar as a group spills out into the parking lot.

"Maybe we should get a drink first?" I attempt to free my hand, but he doesn't release me. His piercing blue eyes bore into mine for a few tense beats, and my insides flutter.

"Thanks for listening and not judging me."

"I'd never judge you. You did what you had to do." My voice lowers, emotion squeezing my throat. "So did I."

"I won't judge you either." He nods, and I believe him.

Kindred spirit.

CHAPTER
SEVEN

ZANE/CHAOS

Words just flowed from my lips like a broken faucet. My dad's death left a curse on my name. My own mother damned me. She rushed to my dad's aid, leaving one of her sons unconscious and the other vibrating with the reality of a life-changing action. When the police asked me why I did it, I said, "Because I hate him."

That hate has never gone away. It festers inside me, fermenting with each passing year. It's a rotting dark stain on my life.

Not her, though. Even with the darkness tormenting her soul, light shines from Lily.

I want to keep her.

I step out of the truck, my boots grinding against

the gravel, and roll my shoulders. Heavy music thrums toward us, getting louder the closer we get to the door. Lily grabs my arm to stop me from going further.

Retching sounds draw our attention to one of the women who just left the bar. She's leaning against the wall, heaving, her friends stumbling and giggling beside her.

"Maybe we get a bottle to go and park somewhere quieter?"

I couldn't agree more. "You go back to the truck. I'll grab us a bottle." I keep my eyes on her until she's back in the truck with the door closed before I head inside.

Trent, the bar owner, spots me immediately and stiffens. A rustle of apprehension tensing his shoulders. It doesn't matter how many times I come drinking here the asshole watches me like I'm going to start fucking shit up.

"All good, Trent?" I ask to be a dick manoeuvring through the crowd to the bar. He offers me pinched features and a grunt. Turning my attention to Willy, one of the bartenders, I ask, "Can I get a bottle of Jack?"

Bodies shove against my back, trying to order drinks by shouting over my shoulder. There's no way Lily and I would have been able to talk over this noise. "Kiss the bride to be?" Some woman croons in my ear, white lace material hanging from her head, a sash across her chest.

"No thanks."

Trent moves from the end of the bar, ushering the people bumping into me farther down. I grin at him, and he nods to Willy, who plonks the bottle on the bar with a glass. "I'll put it on your tab."

"Thanks. I won't be needing this. I'm not staying." I push the glass back toward him, and Trent sags in relief. It's on the tip of my tongue to ask what his problem is but fuck it and fuck him. Lily is waiting.

Swiping up the bottle, I shove my way past everyone until I breathe fresh air again and make my way back to the truck. Lily's in the driver's seat, tapping her thumb on the wheel to the beat of a song on the radio.

Opening the passenger side door, I raise a brow, and she rolls her eyes. "Get in. I want to take you somewhere."

"Should I be worried?"

"You're safe with me." She winks, and it's fucking adorable. Climbing inside, I slam the door closed and buckle in.

Pulling out, she swerves to avoid the group still lingering and merges with traffic. Lights blur past the window, the streets getting quieter as the night wears on. Driving up a suburban street, Lily idles the truck next to an old Toyota.

"This is where I used to live." She points to a one-story house, the garden overgrown with weeds, the paint chipping on the garage door.

"Who lives here now?" I ask, watching her. The light from the moon slices through a break in the clouds, highlighting the side of her face.

"No one," she breathes out, her body almost curling into itself. "I inherited it."

No shit.

"My grandparents inherited me, I suppose, when my mom killed herself." Pain emanates from her in waves.

Fuck, I want to hold her. "Drugs." She scoffs, swiping at her nose, not taking her eyes from the house.

It's an odd-looking place. There's only one window to the side of the house, and the front is just a pale blue wall.

"She must have known what they were." Dropping her hands in her lap, she shivers. "I could have told Jameson. He would have burned this place to ash."

"Why didn't you?" My nerves jitter like bugs have embedded under my skin.

"They got inside my head. Said I was to blame. A dirty little sinner. Told me Jameson would disown me if he knew. Ruby too."

My hand's fist. My muscles coil, stretching my skin. "I couldn't bear the thought of him or Ruby knowing. Still can't." She shakes her head.

"They wouldn't see you differently." Anger boils inside me, needing an outlet. Those motherfuckers hurt her.

"Yes, they would." She turns her gaze to me. "They'd have guilt that they can never get rid of. I'd never do that to them."

"You said you inherited this place, does that mean your grandparents are both dead?" I hope one is alive so I can wrap my hands around their throat and feel the life fade from them.

Opening the truck door, she steps out, and I follow suit.

She walks down the driveway and stops by the windowless wall. Closing her eyes, a single tear falls to her cheek. Her anxiety is palpable, pulsing through my own veins.

What did they do to you?

"They're both dead," she finally says. Taking a deep breath, she smiles to herself before looking back to me. "Because I killed them."

CHAPTER
EIGHT

PAST.

LILY

Eighteen years old…

I shove my clothes into my backpack, feeling energized for the first time in a long time. Jameson got me a job at Hell-made Helmets and said I could stay with him whenever I want.

Eighteen.

I made it.

Getting to my feet, I look around my room, wishing I could burn it to the ground, and close the door behind me. The smell of grandma's pot pie fills the house, turning my stomach to acid. Since I reached sixteen and got my driver's license, I have spent more time out of the house and eating out with Ruby. She noticed the weight I was losing and was concerned I had an eating disorder.

"Where are you going?" My stomach drops at the sound of Grandpa's voice.

Hoisting my bag strap further up my shoulder, I say, "Work."

"Say goodbye to your grandma." He juts his square jaw toward the kitchen, his checked shirt tucked into a pair of gray slacks, the bottom buttons straining to stay closed around his beer belly. I'm tempted to tell him no, but I want to get out of here in one piece.

I walk into the kitchen, and he follows, the scent of Old Spice clinging to the air around me. "Grandma, I'm leaving," I say quickly, looking over my shoulder to see what he's doing. He opens the basement door and disappears down the steps, each thud making me breathe a little easier.

Giving grandma my attention, my brow furrows at the paper in front of her, a little girl's picture clipped to the page, her details written beside it.

Rebecca

Age 9

Foster care for two years.

"What is that?" I ask, a cold whip lashing at my spine.

"Now that you're eighteen, we'll have a room spare."

No. FUCK NO! No.

My fate was sealed by blood. Mother left me to these demons. This child doesn't deserve it.

"Isn't she precious? She looks like you when you came to live with us."

"No." *My backpack drops to the ground as I shake my head, my hair swishing around my face.* "No way."

"What did you say?" She turns to face me, her floral dress making her appear friendly and approachable. It's all a façade.

"I won't let you hurt anyone else." My spine straightens and calm washes over me—an acceptance of what I need to do.

Stop her.

Standing with the help of the table, her crinkly eyes narrow on me. She jabs a chubby finger in my direction. "You'll watch your tone when you're speaking to—"

Her words fall short, her eyes springing wide. I don't realize I've moved until I swing the paddle, colliding with her temple.

Thwack.

The sound is sickening. My whole body shakes as warm, wetness sprays over my face. A red stream paves a path down her cheek. Her skull is in an odd shape, one eye batting like a robot needing to reboot. Pulling my arm back, I hit her again.

Thwack.

A crunch sounds, and she falls with a thud to the tiles at my feet. Blood gushes from a slash in her temple, pooling around her like spilled milk. It expands so fast, I take a step back so it doesn't get on my sneaker.

Breathing heavily, I stare down at the sticky, crimson gore decorating her face.

There's no fear. Only exhilaration courses through my veins.

"Look at you now," I spit out. "You'll never hurt me or anyone else again, you evil fucking bitch." My muscles pull taunt. Tears blur my eyes. My teeth grind. "I fucking hate you!" Emotion churns, pouring out of me without control.

"June, what's going on?"

Shit.

Grandpa's footsteps sound on the stairs. I meet him at the top, and he looks up at me, confused. "Who's screaming?" he asks, like he doesn't know I've finally cracked. He should be used to the sounds of my screams. All I see when I look at him is black coating my skin, infecting my pores, staining my soul. "Where's your grandma?"

He stops two steps from me, his hand on the railing, his eyes focused on my face.

"Is that blood?" He attempts to take another step, but I raise the paddle and bring the edge down on his head. The crack forces one of his eyes to bulge from the socket. It takes effort to tug the paddle free. A squelching sound fills my ears when I manage it. Rouge liquid pours down his face for a few terrifying seconds before he falls backwards, tumbling down the stairs, landing in a heap at the bottom, one leg twisted the wrong way, his arm pinned beneath his frame, the other splayed above his head.

Static fills my mind.

"Grandpa?" My feet carry me down the stairs. The thumping in my chest roars throughout my body. I kick him, but he doesn't move. The paddle drops from my grip,

clanging to the concrete floor by his head. A dent straight down the center of his skull, oozing brain matter, mesmerizes me. One second, two, three…

Movement catches my eye, and I flinch, a cry catching in my throat when his fingers twitch. I look around the space, my eyes landing on their gun cabinet, the key left in the lock. I should have come down here years ago.

There's an old rifle, what looks like a film prop gun, and a small black handheld I take and aim at him. I kick his arm. He doesn't move. Leaning down, I check for a pulse at his wrist.

Nothing.

Blood creates a halo around him, and a disgusting smell wafts into the air, making me gag.

"Lily?" Zane's voice pulls me from my memories, my bones vibrating under my skin. A warm hand grasps mine, entwining our fingers. The sky is a shroud of black, embracing me, promising to keep the secret spoken out loud to another person.

"They wanted to foster a little girl." I close my eyes, squeezing them shut, trying to erase the images I found in boxes in that basement. "I didn't know they fostered before me…before mom. So many kids…" A sob catches in my throat. He drops my hand and pulls me toward him, wrapping me in his embrace. I cling to him, feeling the beat of his heart against mine, the warmth of his body soaking into me, thawing the numbness. "I killed them both—and I enjoyed it. They were evil."

"Are they still in there?" he asks against my ear.

I pull away, frowning, "No. I had help getting rid of them." Ezekiel discovered the bodies when he was hiding out here with my sister Ruby. He didn't ask me questions. He made it look like their car veered off the road down a cliff edge into rocks, the engine exploding, bodies burning.

With a tense jaw, he asks, "So, who is it you want me to help you with?"

My stomach drops, the cold creeping back in, hardening my heart. The obscurity of the night cloaks me, whispering, *"Kill the devil."*

I gulp past the rock in my throat. "Their priest."

CHAPTER
NINE

ZANE/CHAOS

Their priest. Her words ring like a bell clanging against each side of my skull, rattling my brain.

"They would bring him here." She points to the front of the house. "There weren't windows in my room." Lead fills my boots. Every fiber of my being roars with hatred for these strangers.

"No one could hear me cry."

Fuck. I grip her upper arms, my gaze boring deep into her haunted eyes. "You're the only one who will hear him scream when I kill him." Releasing her, I nod my head. "Okay?"

She throws her arms around my neck, jerking me back a step at the force. Before I can register what's happening, her lips crash against mine, hard, punishing, perfect. Then, just as fast, she walks away, back to the truck, leaving me breathless.

Scars are forever, and we're both littered with them, but maybe we can find healing together.

I jog back to the truck and climb in. "Where does he live?"

Her knuckles turn white on the steering wheel. She starts the engine and drives three minutes down the road in silence, pulling up across the street from a church. My mother was religious, but I could never find faith in anything. If there are gods, why do they allow us to suffer so brutally?

"He lives in a house adjacent to the church around the back." She bites on her lip, picking at thread on her jeans.

"Alone?" I ask. Is it priests who have to remain celibate?

"I assume so. I've never seen anyone else come and go."

"How often do you come here?"

"Too often." She begins tapping her foot. "I've killed other people, Zane. We had club business, and it came as easy as pouring myself a drink. But him…" She covers her face with her hands. "Why can't I just do it?"

"Because he fucking traumatized you and we have a natural flight instinct when faced with the perpetrator of that trauma." I grab the bottle of Jack and twist the lid off, handing it to her. "I can't be in the same room as my mother. My skin crawls and rage churns inside me," I grit out. She can't look at me either.

Taking the lid from my hand, she screws the cap back on and chucks the bottle into the backseat before climbing into my lap.

"What are you doing?" I ask, taken aback. Her thighs spread over mine, her pussy grinding down against my cock.

"Let's do something for us. No one controls us." She pants, grasping my face, capturing my lips in her teeth, biting down then sucking. Grabbing her hips, I kiss her back, sweeping my tongue into her mouth and tasting her. Her scent, sweet and mixed with floral notes, invades my senses. She's all around me, intoxicating, then she's gone, back in her seat, mouth red, cheeks flushed, chest heaving.

What the fuck?

"That was nice." She giggles, and I smile over at her, adjusting my hard-on.

"You're a wild one."

"I think you can handle me. Let's get out of here."

"You sure? I can go in right now and end this." I have a blade and a gun in this truck.

"Let's not give him the mercy of a quick kill." There's determination in her eyes.

Fuck. I think I love her.

Starting up the truck, she drives us back to Kirby's

without another word. Parking next to her car, she pulls the keys from the engine and drops them in my palm.

"Why haven't you sold the place?"

Her lips thin as she shakes her head. "Because it's evil.

My prison. No one should have to live there."

"Do you have insurance?"

"Yeah, of course. Why?"

"Because squatters may get in there with it being empty."

"I never thought about that."

Changing the subject, I say, "What you shared with me tonight will never go any further. I know what it cost you to tell me, probably more than most."

"I'll meet you here tomorrow at six and we can scope the club." Before I can reply, she's out of the truck and rounding her car.

A second later, her headlights beam across the lot, and she punches on the gas.

I sit for a few minutes, trying to wrap my head around everything that happened tonight. I glance back, seeing where the bottle of Jack landed, and switch into the driver's seat.

Minutes later, I'm back at her grandparents', parking a few houses away. Grabbing the bottle of Jack, I keep to the shadows and jog to the house, pouring the liquor along the porch and up the front wall. Taking out my lighter, I spark the flame holding it against the wall, watching as the house ignites, burning into the night with an orange glow. It sharply gains momentum, the wood creaking and moaning as it turns black.

"Burn in hell, you motherfuckers."

Soon, their priest will join them.

CHAPTER
TEN

LILY

Walking back into the clubhouse, Rage sniffs my food out like a dog. "You better have something for everyone." He bounds toward me, snatching the fast-food bag from my hands. Opening it up, he looks inside and beams. "This is why you're my favorite."

"I thought it was because I gave you an alibi when you crashed Jameson's bike?"

"That too," he grunts.

A grin spreads up my face as my brother marches up behind him.

"I fucking knew it was you." Jameson snatches the bag from him and helps himself to a burger.

"Fuck." Rage points a finger at me. "Trouble—that's what you are, Lilith."

"You owe me three grand," Jameson informs him.

"Yeah, yeah." Rage narrows his eyes at me and stalks off, taking my food with him.

Lines crease Jameson's forehead.

"You okay?" I ask.

"We just got a call. Your grandparents' place… there's been a fire."

"What?" I bristle. Goosebumps sprinkle over my skin. I was just there.

Zane.

Jameson's warm hand comes down on my shoulder. "I'm sorry, kid. I told you not to leave it sitting empty."

"How bad was the fire?" I cross my arms, not knowing how I feel. Or why I didn't do it years ago.

"They're still there now. It's just happened. You want me to take you?"

"No." I shake my head. "There's no point. I'll go over tomorrow."

"You sure?"

"Yeah, I'm beat. I'm going to crash." I wave a hand and brush past him.

The clubhouse is quiet tonight. The soft thrum of music sets a chill vibe. Some brothers gather around a pool table. Club sluts put on a show, bending over the table and flashing ass while they take a shot. I ignore a couple brothers propped up on the bar, drowning their sorrows, talking about a game their team lost today.

"Where is everyone?" I ask Trixie, a new girl who comes to parties and helps behind the bar.

Her bright blonde hair hangs in ringlets around her shoulders. The bubble gum pink lipstick across her lips glistens under the lights as she says, "A run."

"All of them?"

"Apparently." She shrugs. "You know they don't tell me much." She pops the top off a beer and places it on the bar. "You look like you need this."

"Do I?"

Leaning over the bar, she whispers, "I heard about what happened with Milk. I hate that creep." She winks, sliding the bottle toward me.

"Thanks." Taking the offering, I exit the bar and head down the hall to my room. It took a year for Animal to relent to my whining and give me a place to crash here. The club is overrun with testosterone. Lucky for me, his wife, Drew, is a badass and has been a biker brat her whole life. She agreed we needed more women living here.

Milk rounds the corner, and my feet falter. He freezes, purple and blue bruising marring his face. "Lily…" He nods, ducks his head, and darts past me. Looks like I'm not the only person he pissed off today.

I enter my room, place the beer bottle on my dresser, kick off my boots, and shimmy out of the jeans rubbing against my cut all night. I need to think before acting.

Heading to the floor-length mirror on the back wall, I lift the hem of my panties and hiss, peeling back the small band-aid. Dried blood pulls on the stitches, but thanks to Monroe, the scar will be minimal.

There's a soft knock at the bedroom door before it opens. "Lil, you decent?" Ezekiel calls out, stepping through the threshold.

"A bit late if I wasn't." I raise a brow and chuckle, hurrying over to him and throwing my arms around his neck. "I missed you guys."

"We didn't plan on being gone so long."

He pushes me back and scratches the back of his neck.

"Where's Ruby?" I ask, looking around him for my sister. They went on a run for Animal over two weeks ago.

"She's going to come by tomorrow." He nudges his head toward the door. "I heard about what happened with Milk."

News travels fast. My eyes drop to his hand, and I shake my head. Going over to my dresser, I pull it open, fish a pair of sleep shorts out, and drag them up my legs. "I take it his face is your doing?" I signal toward his bloody knuckles.

"He deserved worse."

"And he got it. I don't need you, Jameson, or Rage fighting my battles."

He scoffs, folding his massive arms over his chest, his muscles pulling his t-shirt taut. "Might not need us but that doesn't mean we won't. You're family. Nothing will ever change that. And I'll be damned if that fucking pervert thinks he can start shit with you and won't catch it from all sides."

"It makes me look weak," I snap, slamming the drawer shut. The beer teeters on the edge as the dresser wobbles.

Taking the drink, Ezekiel tips it to his lips, draining half the bottle before wiping his mouth with the back of his arm and handing me what's left.

"The hole in his hand and the scar it will leave makes you anything but weak, Lil."

"Then why beat the shit out of him?"

"So he fucking learns there's an army at your back. Believe me, I showed restraint because he's a brother."

"Fine. Thanks." I throw my hands up.

Narrowing his eyes on me, he huffs. "You want to tell me what happened to your grandparents' place?"

"The fire?" I ask, lowering myself to my bed. The navy-blue comforter matches the plain painted walls.

There's nothing pink in this room—no soft toys or doll houses. This is my space.

"Is there more than the fire?" he asks, dropping his brow.

"No. Jameson just told me about it, how do you already know?"

"I was there when Animals got the call."

Gulping the beer, I offer a shrug of my shoulders.

"Kids or squatters, I guess. I should have gotten rid of it years ago."

"Where were you tonight?"

Placing the bottle on my bedside table, I chew the inside of my cheek to stop the angry retort wanting to bite at him.

"I'm only asking so I know if there's any damage control I need to deal with."

"I didn't burn the place down, Ezekiel." I roll my eyes and pull the duvet back, slinging it over my bare legs. "If you're done playing dad, I'm tired."

"Don't be a brat. I'm looking out for you, not judging you."

"I didn't burn it down." I puff out an exasperated breath. He stares at me, and I meet his eyes, putting more conviction in my tone. "I didn't."

"Okay. I believe you." He holds up his hands in surrender. "I'll let you get some sleep."

As he turns for the door, I mumble, "Ezekiel…" he stills but doesn't turn around, "thanks for always looking out for me."

"You don't need to thank me. We're family."

Emotion clogs my throat. "Hug Ruby for me, yeah?"

"You can hug her yourself tomorrow."

The door closes with a soft click, and my body runs cold. Jumping up, I rush over and turn the handle, making sure it opens, my heart hammering against my ribcage. A slight breeze billows in, and my limbs relax.

Shutting it again, I back up until my legs hit my bed. Ezekiel cares about me, and I have a family, but every night, I sleep with the light on and the door unlocked, my secrets sheltered away, rotting me from the inside out.

CHAPTER
ELEVEN

ZANE/CHAOS

"Leo, you up?" I call out when I get back to his house. Every light is on. The place practically glows from the outside.

He appears from the dining room, shirtless, blonde hair sticking up all over his head, a rag in his hand. "I'm up."

"What are you doing?"

"Cleaning the mess." I've been gone for hours. Cleaning shouldn't have taken that long. "Is Lily okay?" He looks around, expecting to see her with me.

"She's fine. Went back to the clubhouse, I think. It's late. You should try to get some rest."

"I can't sleep." He scrubs his hands down his face and paces the kitchen.

"You want me to crash here tonight?" Opening the fridge, I grab a carton of leftover Chinese from last night.

"No, I'm good." He smacks his hand against his thigh, soap dripping from his hand to the floor, avoiding eye contact.

"Well, I'm going to watch some TV for a bit then I'll go home." He's agitated and won't settle for hours. I shouldn't have left him earlier.

"Can you tell me when you're going to get Kelly?" he asks, following me into the living room.

"Tomorrow evening." I don't know if we'll execute the plan tomorrow, but we'll be making one after visiting the club.

"I have this fucking feeling she's dead." He scrunches his face, shaking his head.

"Leo…" I dump the Chinese food on the coffee table and grasp his shoulders, trying to anchor him so he doesn't spiral, "she's fine. Soon, you'll be off living life together. Breathe."

Taking a couple deep breaths, he jerks his head. "Yeah, you're right." Sniffing me, he asks, "Why do you smell like smoke?"

I lift my shirt to my nose, shrugging. "Not important."

Finally bringing his eyes to mine, he holds me there for a few seconds before blinking. "Okay. I'm going to go lay down."

"Good. I'll be right here." I point to the couch I'm not looking forward to crashing on.

"Okay." He disappears up the stairs. Despite this place having three bedrooms, I'll never step foot on that staircase. I know Leo left it all untouched.

A picture of the past.

A museum.

Memories assault me. Hearing my mother cry. The sound of my dad kicking the shit out of her. The wait for the bedroom handle to drop when he needed someone else to beat.

Leo getting out of here will do him a world of good. The moment he takes off with Kelly, I'll burn this place to the ground too.

Toeing off my boots, I throw my ass onto the couch and turn the volume up on the TV, re-runs of an old show flicking on the screen. Lily fills my head. Her story is so fucking dark, yet she came out on the other side, damaged but teeming with this life force I want to wrap myself in it.

The floorboard whines and creaks above my head as Leo paces his bedroom floor. It's going to be a long night. Punching the sofa cushion, I put my head down and close my eyes for a second.

"Why did you do it!" Mom screams. Blood coats her hands. Her face distorts. She's coming closer.

"Why did you put her out there?" Her voice is now a whisper. *"Why?"*

I jolt awake, my hands thrown up in defense. A shadow lingers over me. Startled, I scurry backward.

"Mom?" I croak, my voice still strained from sleep.

"Why did you do it?" the figure asks. I rub my eyes. Nope, still fucking there. Jumping to my feet, I stumble away from the thin, straggly-haired woman with my mother's face.

"I don't want to see her," she cries.

"Leo," I call up the stairs, my skin crawling. "Leo!" I bark.

Movement sounds, and he appears at the top of the stairs, stark naked, holding a gun. "What's wrong?"

"Mom's here." A chill blows in from the wide-open front door, carrying leaves in with it.

Thudding down the stairs, Leo frowns, shaking his head at me. "Did you say Mom?" Following my stare, he slaps the gun against my chest, dropping it and going over to her.

"Mom, how the hell did you get out of there?" He sits her down and pulls a blanket from the back of a chair, wrapping it around his waist.

"Meadow Fields?" I scratch the back of my neck pinching there to make sure I'm not asleep.

"I've been detoxing her here."

Leo confesses and my brain explodes. "What the fuck, Leo?"

"No. I'm not going back there, I see her." Her words

gain in pitch, and she pushes Leo away. We haven't seen each other in almost two years. By the looks of her, you'd think it's been twenty. Her hair is gray. Stress lines cut into her features. There's a tooth missing in the front row of her mouth. She's a mess.

"She needs real doctors. Look at her." I scoff.

"It's cold down there." The woman is delusional.

"They have doctors there, Leo. You can't fucking help her here. Where the hell have you been keeping her?"

"Upstairs, she tries to get out." My gaze cuts to the front door. She must have seen me and changed her plan.

"I'm not going back," she mumbles. Her eyes finding mine, she jabs a thin finger toward me. "Why did you do it?"

Every fucking time she sees me, that's all she asks. "Because he was a piece of shit," I snarl.

She flinches, reaching out for Leo, and he goes to her, a softness in his gaze I'll never understand. "Come on, Mom. I'll take you back upstairs."

"No Leo. She needs real care. They will come and get her." There's no room for argument in my tone.

I watch him wrestle with the idea, his eyes flitting between us. "Fine. But I'll take her there."

"You going to put some clothes on first?"

"Are you going to watch her while I do?"

For fuck's sake. "Just be quick."

"Don't leave me with him, Leo. He'll kill me too."

"I'm not the fucking monster here, woman," I growl, wanting to shake sense into her.

"No he won't. Just sit down while I get some clothes on."

After she takes a seat, he marches over to me. "She's fragile. Don't be a dick. I'll be two minutes." Snatching the gun from me, he bounds up the stairs two at a time.

Once he's out of sight, she darts her gaze around the place, twisting her lips. "I don't like it here. It's all wrong."

"No one asked you to come back here," I grunt, going to the kitchen and pouring a glass of water from the faucet. A shadow darts toward the front door in my peripheral. "Fuck." I chase her down the steps, almost slipping in mud when she starts across the small piece of greenery straight into the street and onto the road.

Slowing my pace, she stops and stands there glaring at me, I place my hand on my hips. "Get out of the road."

"Why did you do it, Zane?" She rubs at her arms, her collarbone protruding, her eyes sunken in. Why couldn't she have loved us more than she did him. Look what loving him got her. Headlights beam coming over the hill. It would take nothing to let her die right now. Let the metal plough into her erasing the bitter hag. Let her rot in hell with dad if she misses him that much. My heart rate soars, pounding in my ears as the lights get closer. A squeal from her lips shatters the night, and I jolt into action

Racing forward, I sweep her out of the way just as the horn blares and the car swerves. Breathing erratically, she wiggles from my hold. "Don't touch me."

I grit my teeth, jabbing a finger right back at her. "I killed him because if I hadn't, he would have killed you. Worse—he could have killed Leo. Someone had to protect us—and it should have been you."

"What happened?" Leo barks, hurrying over to us.

"It's cold down there." She mumbles.

"Nothing. Just take her back. I'm going home."

"You're not losing it, Leo. Take a deep breath." I rub my eyes, a yawn forcing its way out of me.

"The dream was so real," he repeats down the line.

"You shouldn't be sleeping through the day. That's

why you're up all night." Another car pulls into Kirby's, but it's not Lily. She's twenty minutes late, and I'm kicking myself for not taking her number.

"Fuck that. I sleep when I can. She's dead. I know it."

"Why would they kill her?" Maybe if she stole from them, but men like Ronaldo would rather put a woman like Kelly to work to recoup the money she took.

"I see her buried in the mud. It's so clear. It's all over me."

"Leo. Calm down. It's the nightmare and everything that happened with Mom. Your mind is fucking with you."

"I should be there helping you."

Pinching the bridge of my nose, I tell him, "It's not safe for both of us to go in."

"Then it should be me. They can't hurt me. It should be me."

"You need to get your stuff together. Once she's out, you're going to need to be ready."

"Right. You're right. Shit. Okay."

"Okay?"

"Yeah, I'm going to pack a bag."

Lily's car pulls into the spot next to me, and relief settles in my chest. I end the call with Leo as Lily steps out of the car. My mouth goes dry, and my dick jerks to life. "Fuck." She's wearing a tight black dress that clings to her body like saran wrap. No bra. Pebbled nipples. My balls ache at the sight.

Opening the truck door, I whistle, and she curtsies, the fabric raising up her thighs, giving me a glimpse of her lace panties. "I thought I better dress the part," she says, gesturing down her body. Her hair is pulled into some updo, and it draws my attention to her long, slender neck. I want to bite it.

"Are you sure you want to do this?" Every fucking mouth in that club will drop when she walks in looking like a snack.

Rolling her eyes, she rounds the truck, pulls open the passenger door, and maneuvers herself inside with ridiculous heels on. Fuck, her legs go on for miles. "Impressive." I nod.

"The outfit or me being able to climb in wearing it?"

"Both." I grin.

Definitely the outfit.

CHAPTER
TWELVE

LILY

"I expected a more barn-looking structure with titty lights and all that jazz." The hem of my dress keeps rising, and I regret asking Trixie to lend it to me. Nothing in my closet would get me in those doors, though, so I have to suck it up.

"Apparently, it's a classy joint." Zane guffaws. In dark jeans and a fitted tee, his hair pulled back in a low ponytail, saliva floods my mouth looking at him.

"Have you been here before?" I ask, scanning the place.

The outside is a sleek black box with a purple light flashing "FLESH." There's a silhouette of a woman bending over and blowing a kiss, kinda like tinker bell without wings.

"No, I haven't been here. Leo has."

"Is that how he met Kelly?"

"With him, fuck knows."

"Do you have to be a member?" I ask, pulling down the hem of the dress once more, drawing Zane's gaze to the action. He swipes his tongue out to wet his lips, shuffling in his seat, and my lower stomach pools with need.

"Not for the main club," he grunts.

"Why couldn't you or Leo just join the sex club and get in that way?"

"It's invite only. Exclusive." He looks me over, his jaw ticking. "You sure you want to do this?"

"Are you? That's like the fourth time you've asked me."

Instead of answering, he pushes the door open, climbs out, and comes to my side to help me down.

"So, how do we play this?" I ask, making sure my boob tape is keeping the girls in place.

"What do you mean?"

"Well, are we friends looking for lap dances or a couple spicing things up? We need a back story. It helps." I shrug.

"Horney couple, I guess." He grins wickedly.

"Speak for yourself." My gaze drops to his crotch before I waltz past him to the club entrance.

Black marble tiles from floor to ceiling make up the foyer. Thin purple strobe lights border the walls, giving a subtle glow. Two bouncers stand by a large door, their hands bigger than my head. A pretty blonde sits behind the counter, talking to the guys who walked in before us.

She stamps their hands, but no ink shows. They move toward the door, and the bouncer sweeps them with a metal detector before letting them pass. Zane walks up to the desk and says, "Two."

"Fifty for you. Thirty for your girlfriend," the woman tells him.

Fishing out a stack of bills from his back pocket, Zane drops a hundred on the counter. "Keep the change."

"Thanks," the smile she offers him is damn right lustful. Grasping his hand, she takes her time pushing the inker into his skin and then stamps mine with a quick flick of her wrist. "Have fun." She purrs.

The bouncers wave their metal detectors over us, and my stomach drops when it beeps over Zane. Digging into his pocket, he pulls out a metal lighter and shows them the cause. They look between themselves and then jerk their chin for him to move aside and turn their focus on me, patting my body down. Their hands on me make me want to gut them both.

"Maybe buy me a drink before grouping me." I snap.

"Go ahead." The doors open, and sultry music pours through, matching the beat of my heart. I shrug to Zane and head down a stairs, walking straight into a club. "That was easy enough."

"Were you worried they would card you?" He raises a brow, his gaze sweeping over my body.

Actually, that hadn't crossed my mind.

Stepping further inside, a smile spreads up my face. It's not too different from the clubhouse when they host parties for other chapters. Women twirl and grind on poles on a raised dancefloor. A bar runs in an L shape along the back wall. Mirrored ceilings give the illusion of endless space and views from all angles. Men from all walks of life fill the tables, with beautiful dancers grinding on them up close and personal—skin to skin. My eyes trail to the top floor. A large office overlooks the bar. A spiral staircase leads to the entrance, another giant guarding the route up.

Ronaldo must feel real macho up there. I snort a laugh.

"What's funny?"

"How trashy and lame this guy must be."

"He feeds on the fact that he's related to an Aire. It makes him feel untouchable." Zane narrows his eyes on the bouncer.

"Why surround himself with muscle if he feels untouchable?" I jut my chin toward the bar. "Let's get a drink."

Zane leans over to the bar and curls his finger toward the bartender. "Two beers," he tells him, dropping money down, earning an appreciative smile.

"He likes you," I tease, looking over my shoulder at the guy's ass in a pair of black leather slacks.

"Everything with a pulse likes me, Lily. I'm pretty."

I bark a genuine laugh then swig the beer he hands me, tilting my head toward him. "You certainly are. Maybe you should have worn this dress."

"Nah, it doesn't match my shoes."

I knock my shoulder into his, biting my lip. After such heavy confessions last night, it's nice that we can be ourselves. I've never had that. The ink from the stamps glow now we're surrounded by black lights. The word FLESH glares up at me.

"Let's get a table." Taking my hand, he leads me to the far end of the club, away from crowd. The warmth of his palm in mine sends butterflies jumping around my stomach.

I like and hate it.

The contradiction sits heavy in my chest. It fills intimate holding hands. I like to be in control when it comes to men and sex and who I allow to touch me. Stomach flutters and heart palpitations whenever he looks at me isn't control.

Holding out my chair for me, I sit and survey the office while sipping my beer. The space is on full show, illuminated by a bright hanging chandelier hovering above a desk in the centre of the room. A heavy-set bald man is sitting at it. Cabinets span the wall behind him a set of metal doors are to his right. Another man enters via the staircase. He's wearing a black suit like the bouncers at the door. He touches his earpiece, and a conversation ensues with the bald man waving his arms around like a conductor. You don't have to hear the conversation to know the poor bastard is getting an earful.

Leaning into Zane, I ask, "Is that Ronaldo?"

Following the path of my gaze, Zane shifts in his seat, his tongue swiping out to dampen his lips, making need build in my womb. He's so close I can taste the beer on his breath.

"Yeah. Overseeing the club makes him feel like a king, no doubt."

"More like a fucking idiot." I scoff.

Chuckling, he leans back into my space, and my body wants to close the gap and give in to the lust coursing through me.

"Kelly said he often brings girls up from the sex club and fucks them over his desk."

"Pig." My hand tightens around the beer bottle. "Must mean there's an entrance to the sex club in here, though, right?"

He subtly motions to the right of the room, where a second set of steel doors stand out. "An elevator?" I gasp, whipping my head back up to the office. The metal doors are in the same place.

"Kelly said it covers all floors, but it's not for public use."

"Maybe we try to call it and see what happens?" those blue eyes of his snare me and my brain forgets how to function. Men shouldn't be allowed to be as pretty as him. It's unfair.

"From what I can see there's no call button. It must be a key or code."

"Why don't I mingle and ask some of the girls if they've seen Kelly?" I need some space or I'm going to climb into his lap and become the entertainment.

Placing his hand on my arm, he says, "Is that a good idea?"

"Do you have a better one?"

"I was thinking we need to get in that elevator." He hasn't removed his hand and the skin beneath it burns traveling up my arm and crawling up my neck.

"There has to be another way. There's probably a back entrance. Let's make sure she's definitely down there first."

"Okay. I'll hang back here and keep an eye on Ronaldo."

"At least get a dance from one of the girls so you don't stand out." Getting to my feet, I pass a slim brunette wearing a jewelled bikini with nipple tassels defying gravity. Biting her lip, she twirls her hair and acts coy as I approach.

"My friend over there would love you to give him a dance," I tell her, pointing to Zane.

When he notices what I'm doing, he narrows his eyes on me, and I grin. "Mmm, no problem."

"Oh…" I stop her from leaving and whisper into her ear, "and tell him your name's Lily."

CHAPTER
THIRTEEN

ZANE/CHAOS

The dancer's hair swishes across my face as she grinds her ass on my cock, getting stuck to my lip. "We don't have a no-hands policy," she croons over her shoulder. "You can touch." Spreading her thighs, she runs her hands up them, teasing the line of her panties. I place my hand under her tit and squeeze, and her fake moan makes my balls want to shrivel up.

Getting to her feet, she straddles me, moving like a pro over my cock, her tits rubbing against my chin. "I'm Lily." The words come out low and throaty.

I peer into her green eyes, looking for the lie. She's attractive, there's no denying that, but she's not who I want sitting on my dick. Shifting her off my lap, I pull out some cash from my back pocket and hand it to her. "Why don't you go get us some drinks?"

There's no way that's a coincidence. Lily must have told her to say that. She's playing games, wanting me thinking about her while getting my dick teased. We don't need games for that. I've been thinking about her since last night. The heat of her pussy on my lap…her tongue tangling with mine…

Fuck, now my cock's getting hard.

"Okay?" the dancer questions, her brow pulling down, her lips thinning.

I scan the club, finding Lily almost immediately. Encircled by men and women, and damn, the girl stands out. She's stunning, and I'm jealous of those fuckers getting that smile. Her laughter carries through the music, hitting me square in the chest as I stalk her. Jealously tangles with rationality, "You can't kill them for making her laugh, Zane." I tell myself. That woman is under my skin, drawing me closer. Her resilience and fire can bring any man to his knees, and if she asked me to, I'd drop to mine in an instant. Side-sweeping a barmaid, I get closer to Lily, ready to whisk her away back to our table. I want her to myself.

"Hey, gorgeous. You all alone?" a blonde asks, her tits on display. "I do private dances." She licks her lips, groping her own tits. I'm six feet from Lily. I don't want to let her out of my sight, but we're here to do a job.

"Where?" I ask, and she smiles, holding out her

hand. "I'll show you." This may be a way into the club below. Taking her hand, I let her guide me through the club to a doorway near the stairs where we came in. Lily's eyes track my departure, and I offer a subtle nod.

"This way," the blonde purrs, sashaying her ass as she leads me down a hall of numbered doors, taking me inside room five. Heat smacks me in the face as we enter. Sweat clings to the air, sticking to my skin. If you can call it a room. More like a closet. A black box with a pole running from the center to the ceiling.

Pushing me into the purple half-moon bench on the back wall, she points to a camera. "It's for my protection. They watch but don't listen. If you want me to talk dirty, I can."

If someone's going to be watching, what does it matter if they listen? "You can touch my tits—not my pussy. I can give you a hand job, but no blow jobs."

Fuck, how many cocks have cum on this seat? That's probably what I'm inhaling.

"I heard I can get the full experience." I slump back and grab my junk to show interest.

Wagging her finger, she steps up to the pole and spins around it. "Not in this club. You mean Bare Flesh. It's members only. You shouldn't even know about it." She curls her leg around the pole and slides all the way down, spreading her legs once hitting the black box.

"Well, when the pussy is good, men like to talk about it." I wink.

"It's a kink club. What's your flavor?" Her tits

bounce with her movements as she gets into a kneeling position.

"Do you ever work down there?" I flick my tongue out to wet my lips, and her eyes follow the action.

Tutting, she steps down, spreads my thighs wider apart, and shimmies up my body. "The girls who work that club are trained in their field."

"Fucking?" I ask. Agitation ignites in her eyes.

"It's a kink club, each worker is a professional and trained." Her tone has lost the sultry purr. "Do you want a hand job or what?"

"Listen," I lean into her ear and stuff a couple hundreds into her G-string, "I usually come here to see a particular girl, Kelly, but she hasn't been in and someone mentioned her moving to the club downstairs."

Turning her head, her lips almost brush mine. I'm thankful she doesn't suck dick in here. "Kelly hasn't shown up for work. We've been trying to reach her." A line slashes across her forehead.

"Maybe she's been moved to the other club?" I pry.

"No." She stands and crosses her arms, her tits resting on them. "Kelly's a pole girl. She doesn't even do private dances."

A knock comes at the door, and a deep voice calls out, "You good in there, Goldie?"

"Yeah, fine. I think this guy prefers brunettes." Turning on her heel, she opens the door. "We're done here," she announces, gesturing with her hand for me to leave.

"Thanks for the dance." I ignore the bouncer glaring at me as I pass through the hallway back to the main bar just in time to see Lily being led up the stairs to Ronaldo's office by two men.

Fuck.

CHAPTER
FOURTEEN

LILY.

"Who does your nails? Mine are horrendous." I hold back my gag as I ask the question to the bartender bringing over an order of drinks. I've never painted my nails in my life, but I've heard club sluts talking at the clubhouse.

"Diamond Jewels on Harrison Road. Whitney— she's the best." Handing me a beer bottle, her gaze travels my body. "I love your dress. You could kill it here in tips if you ever need a job." She winks.

"Actually, my friend works here. I was hoping to see her." I keep my tone casual, shifting my gaze around the room.

"Oh really?" She hands out some more of the drinks, but her attention is set on me.

"Yeah, her name's Kelly." She almost drops the glass she's holding.

"Kelly Lorre?" she asks, concern tugging on her brow.

"Yeah, we went to school together." I shrug, swigging from the bottle. The cold liquid sloshes in my stomach.

"She hasn't been in all week."

"Oh, is she sick?" I place a hand on my chest.

"I couldn't tell you. The boss doesn't tell us anything. Enjoy the drink." She spins around and walks off taking some of the drinks with her.

A guy lurking around me throws his hands up. "My beer?"

There's a group of them for a bachelor's party. Stepping into my personal space, he drags his lustful gaze over me. "What's the cost for a dance?"

"Your life if you don't get out of my face." I shove his shoulders, and he stumbles back, knocking into one of the girls entertaining another table. An older guy topples from his chair, and a chorus of yelling back and forth ensues.

Two bouncers appear, and I grin, hoping I'm about to watch the little pervert get thrown out—preferably with a fight. The two men stop before me, blocking my view with their mammoth frames. "Gentlemen, you make better doors than windows."

"Boss wants to see you," one of them states.

"Do my tits look like they're out?" I snap,

attempting to get around them. They're pros and prevent me from leaving. "I don't work here, assholes."

"We don't care where you work. You're coming with us."

"And if I don't?"

"Don't make a scene and we won't have to," he grunts, grabbing my arm.

"Manhandling me will get you a scene. A bloody one," I growl. Taking my beer from me, the one yet to speak gestures to my arm with his head, and the brute releases me with a huff. My skin stings, but I won't show him it hurts. Folding my arms, I cock a brow.

"Well, take me to him then."

I glance over my shoulder, trying to spot Zane, as I follow them, not seeing him anywhere. He must still be with that stripper. A small whirling of jealousy pangs my stomach.

Curious eyes watch and murmur as we pass through the club. "Up the stairs."

Hairs rise on the back of my neck, and I sense Zane watching me. My gaze finds his just before I go inside the room. I manage to shake my head no, trying to tell him not to come for me. *Let this play out.*

The lesser asshole ushers me inside with his meaty palm on my back.

Ronaldo doesn't get up from his desk. In a suit he's squeezed his fat into, he looks like a villain from an old movie, chuffing on a cigar, a glass of amber liquid on his desk. "Hello, sweetheart," he greets me, and my skin crawls. His gaze is outright obscene, like he can see through my clothes and fantasizes about touching the flesh beneath. "You've been asking questions about Kelly?"

Fucking bartender.

"I know her and heard she's a dancer here." I shrug my shoulders.

"Is that so?"

"Is there a problem with that?" I ask, attempting to keep the challenge from my tone.

The leather of his seat creaks as he stands, and I have to bite the inside of my cheek to prevent myself from laughing as Penguin comes to mind. I close my eyes to get a handle on myself. He's really fucking short.

"Kelly hasn't shown up for work this week."

Taking a breath, I focus on a spot next to him. "Maybe she's sick."

"The girl stole from me. There's no doubt she skipped town."

The energy in the room shifts, almost with a crackle. Ronaldo's hands fist, and he leans against the lip of the desk. "I'm going to gut her when I do find her."

A cold chill dusts my skin. My heartbeat picks up its pace.

"I was told she was in your private club." I decide to forgo the bullshit.

"Is that so? And was it a blonde drug addict who told you that?"

"What?" My nerves bounce around under my skin.

"Leo Bridgemen—Kelly's plaything," he grunts, gesturing to the guy who brought me in here. Moving behind the desk, the guy taps his fingers over the keyboard and lifts the laptop, carrying it over to me.

My stomach bottoms out when I see Leo's house on the screen.

"I have someone watching the house in case Kelly shows up, and guess who visited Leo on the back of his brother's bike?" A bark of laughter, sinister and deep, rattles his chest. "It's funny." He points to me, his cigar clutched between his forefinger and thumb. The scent fills the room, a toxic cloud billowing toward me, making me cough. I want to vomit. It feels like the pig is inside me, crawling around under my skin. "That's not where I recognize you from, though."

"Oh yeah?" Horror floods my veins, and I think back to the boxes my grandparents kept in the basement. So many indecent images. I don't remember them ever taking pictures of me, but they drugged me a lot. I always feared there could be some of me out in the world.

"You're a Royal Bastard," he states, and my head swims. "I've been to the clubhouse, seen you there." Gesturing down my body, he chuckles, "Though, you didn't look like this."

"Is Kelly here or not?" My patience is thin. Thinking

about those monsters and being around this one puts me on edge. Sweat beads on my forehead, anxiety kicking in.

"I already told you I'm looking for her too." He narrows his round brown eyes. "Kelly was good for the pole but weak-willed. She wouldn't be able to handle the private club." What a scumbag. "I can tell by your face you disapprove," he tuts. Getting to his feet, he walks over to the drink cabinet and takes a bottle of whiskey out, topping off his glass.

"No, it sounds delightful," I scoff.

"You want to see for yourself?" Dark, hairy brows raise like caterpillars on his face.

"Are you going to let me leave after?"

Holding out his hands, he chuckles, making his suit jacket almost burst open. "I'm a businessman, not a savage."

He's forgetting he just threatened to gut Kelly.

"Rylie, take Lily down in the elevator." My mouth pops open as my name leaves his lips.

If he notices my surprise, he doesn't say anything. Rylie takes my upper arm but doesn't apply pressure like the brute downstairs. "Sure thing, boss."

"Don't have too much fun down there, Lily. Your brother won't like me keeping you." His dark laughter follows us into the elevator. When the doors close, my heart accelerates.

I'm fucked.

If he doesn't kill me, Jameson will.

CHAPTER
FIFTEEN

ZANE/CHAOS.

"How was it?" some frat boy-looking kid asks as I stop near a table. He's sitting with a group of guys who can barely be in their twenties.

"What?" I try to keep my attention on Lily, my mind racing.

Motioning to something behind me, he says, "The private dance—is it worth it?"

"Sure, kid. If you want an STD."

"Tequila!" someone yells as a bartender saunters over, placing down shot glasses. "She let you fuck her?" he asks, bewilderment glassing his eyes.

Lily doesn't look scared. Defiance masks her features. Ronaldo keeps chuckling, making me want to knock his teeth out.

We were supposed to devise a plan to do this quietly. By the looks of it, I'll be going the chaos route.

When one of the bouncers starts leading Lily to the elevator, I nudge my knee into the table, spilling the round of drinks.

"Dude!" The frat boy darts to his feet, liquid coating the table and dripping over the edge into his lap. Keeping my eyes glued to the elevator doors, my chest begins to pound. It's not stopping.

They're taking her to Bare Flesh.

I slip my lighter from my pocket, ignoring the angry guys telling me I have to buy another round, I ignite the flame, and set the table on fire.

"Shit! Fire!" a woman dancing on the stage yells. Screams fill the air as I flip the table over and march toward the stairs.

Catching a bouncer approaching me from the left in my peripheral, I swipe two beer bottles from a table and crack them together, shattering the bases, leaving me with two jagged edges. Ronaldo and a big mother-fucker look down through the window. Ronaldo starts hollering, waving his arms around. A second later, the big cunt comes out the door toward the stairs.

Swerving around toppled-over chairs, I launch myself at the bouncer coming from the left. With quick movements, I avoid a blow he swings at me and jab one of the bottles into his armpit.

Stab, stab.

When he falls forward, confused, I jam the second

bottle into his neck and maneuver under the staircase, grabbing the ankles of the beast coming down them through the gap. His heavy momentum causes him to fall hard. A gun clatters down with him, sliding beneath a table. Shouting and screaming drown out the soft music as people scatter like rats.

Jumping over the bouncer bleeding out with the bottle in his jugular, I duck beneath the table to get the gun, but someone pulls on my foot, dragging me from beneath the table. Rearing my other leg back, I ram it forward into his face. Blood pours from a cut on his brow. He staggers backwards, giving me time to grab a chair and get to my feet. I smash him with it once, twice. The wood splinters, coming away in my hands —three, four—until I'm pelting him with just a leg. The bastard is strong. Cracking the leg against his temple dazes him, and he wobbles on his feet.

I hit him again.

Five, six.

His skull is an odd shape. Blood gushes from his nose, lips, and ears. Wheezing and mumbling, he falls, cracking his face on the raised dancefloor.

I launch for the gun as two more bouncers rush through the club, pulling their own weapons and shooting. A bullet embeds in the table, making me flinch.

Close one.

A shrill alarm blares through the room, and water bursts from the ceiling like rain.

Wrapping my palm around the gun handle, I wait for footsteps to stall then pop out and shoot, hitting one right in the forehead and the other in the shoulder. "Shit," he barks, trying to lift his arm to aim at me, but the bullet prevents his movement.

Walking toward him, water soaking me to the core, I blast two to his chest, dropping him instantly. Sprinklers begin to tame the flames from getting higher. Smoke fills the room. A rush of people try to flee. Glancing up at the office, I see Ronaldo banging his fist against the elevator door. The elevator has a trigger to stop working when the alarm goes off. Too dangerous. Unlucky for Ronaldo.

Taking the steps up two at a time, I barge into his office. The runt races around his desk, almost slipping in the water puddling on the floor. He holds his hands up in surrender. The arrogant little shit doesn't even have a weapon. He thought he would be safe up here with his little army of giants. Pathetic.

"Kelly isn't here," he grumbles.

"Where is Lily?" I growl, stalking him.

"She's safe as long as I am." Banging comes from the elevator, and I shift around the desk, grabbing Ronaldo by the lapel of his jacket with my free hand.

"Sit the fuck down." I shove him into his seat and aim the gun at the elevator doors.

"Do you know who I am?" the weasel cries out.

"A piece of shit?" I sneer. "Is there no other way out of here?" I ask, scanning the room for an exit.

"No. The elevator and stairs are the only way in and out."

The water suddenly shuts off, and I shake my head to clear my eyes.

"You're both going to pay for this. My family will butcher you."

"Shut up." More banging and metal groaning.

The doors crack open a slither, then fingers poke through, pushing it wider. My heart soars.

Lily.

CHAPTER
SIXTEEN

LILY

"Kelly isn't working at Bare Flesh," Rylie announces as the elevator descends. "She's a manipulator and a thief."

"Know her well?" I ask, my eyes roaming over his face.

The muscles in his jaw twitch, and he clasps his hands in front of him. "If she's ghosted Leo, it's because she found another idiot to take her in."

"You sound bitter."

"Bitter would mean I give a shit. I don't."

"Who are you trying to convince?" I scoff as the doors ping. He shoves me forward, and I snap, "Don't push me asshole."

"What are you going to do—hit me with your purse?"

"I don't have a purse, but I have fists and teeth."

"Are you trying to scare me or turn me on?"

We round a corner, and my mouth drops. Various platforms border a club floor, sex acts being performed by couples and groups on them. Booths surround the stages with raised backs for privacy. A circular bar sits in the center. All the bartenders are fully naked, barring a small black mask over their eyes. Rylie leans in and murmurs into my ear, "No one is forced to perform down here. They beg to."

A soft pulse vibrates the floor and sets my blood bubbling. "Come on."

He tugs me toward a door, stopping abruptly when an alarm blasts over the music. "What's going on?" I ask, looking around.

"Fire." He frowns, clutching my arm. He drags me back the way we came to the elevator and forces me inside with him. Hitting the button, the doors close. We start to ascend, only to stall as the elevator jolts to a stop.

"What the fuck?" I hate small, enclosed spaces. Panic flares inside me.

"The sprinkler system must have been activated." He bashes the buttons, growling when nothing happens.

"If the sprinklers went off, that means it's a real fire, right?"

Zane.

Looking around the small square tin, he nods to the ceiling. "There's a latch. I'll lift you."

"And then what?"

"See how far we are from the doors."

"If this starts up again and I get squashed, I'm coming back to fucking haunt you."

He attempts to wrap his arms around my thighs, and I smack him away. "Use your hands to make a step. No grabbing the goods."

"Get over yourself. I prefer more meat on the bone."

"Fuck you. I worked hard for the meat I have."

Interlocking his fingers, he holds them out for me. I kick off my heels and grab his shoulders, stepping into his hands with one foot, knowing he's getting a view straight up my dress when he boosts me up.

He lifts me with ease, and I fiddle with the lock, pushing the latch open. I hoist my body through the small gap. Thick metal cables surround me, keeping the elevator suspended. The shaft is just concrete blocks and cables. A fire shouldn't spread in here. The metal doors are right in front of me, and I hear voices on the other side.

"What do you see?" Rylie calls up.

"They're right here," I shout back, attempting to pry the doors open. I smack my palm against them when they don't budge.

"I can't open them." I hold my hands out, looking down the gap to where Rylie stands.

"I'm not fitting through that." He frowns. "I'll give you something to help you open them, but you have to promise you'll tell someone I'm down here."

"What do you have?" I look over the black suit he's wearing. There's no way he's hiding something on him.

"You better not fuck me over." Gritting his teeth, he turns and opens a panel under the buttons on the elevator wall. There's a fire extinguisher and a small axe. "Promise me you'll get help," he demands.

"Promise." My tone is solid, believable. He holds up the hatchet, and I lean into the hole to grip it. Snatching my wrist, he almost tugs me back inside. "Rylie," I warn, my breathing ragged. I attempt to steady myself with my free hand, but he's strong.

"I have a family. Don't leave me here if this place is on fire."

"I won't."

He releases me, and I shove away from the hole, getting to my feet. Taking a couple calming breaths, I adjust my grip on the hatchet and jam the blade into the crease of the doors, pushing all my weight into the handle. Metal creaks and groans, and suddenly, the doors give way. "It's working." Relief pours into my veins.

"Keep going."

I throw more of my weight into the handle, and it

wedges open enough for me to get my hands through. Placing the hatchet down, I pry with my hands, forcing the space to become big enough for me to fit through. Picking the weapon back up, I squeeze through the doors.

"Lily." Zane's relieved voice coats me in a cloak of joy. He's soaking wet, his tee clinging to him, showing his toned physique beneath.

"You're both dead," Ronaldo spits, smacking his fist on the desk from his chair. Zane aims his gun at him, and I shake my head and raise the hatchet, launching it toward Ronaldo. Zane darts out of the way and it lands with a thud in Ronaldo's chest, his chair scooting a few inches back. His eyebrows raise. His eyes spring wide, mouth drops open. Blood leaks from his lips as his head lulls.

"Lily?" Rylie's voice echoes through the gap in the doors as Zane rushes toward me, grabs the back of my head with his palm, and slams his mouth to mine. Rough and full of need, I cling to him, tangling my tongue with his, tasting him.

Pulling away, he grins. "Let's get out of here."

"Lily…" Rylie calls again. "Lily!"

"Who is that?" Zane frowns, trying to see through the space.

"No one. Let's go."

CHAPTER
SEVENTEEN

ZANE/CHAOS

Flashing lights illuminate the sky as we exit the club. Fire trucks and cop cars are parked out front. Crowds of people fill the parking lot, making it easy for Lily and me to blend in as we maneuver our way to my truck.

"Sprinkler system works," Lily points out, a wild spark in her eyes. A pink tinge warms her cheeks as she beams a smile.

God, she's beautiful.

"Honestly, I expected someone to put it out with a fire extinguisher." The fire was completely out by the time we passed through the club, but the water damage is going to be far worse.

"Look," Lilly murmurs. I follow her gaze, my brow

furrowing. A cop is attempting to stop cars from leaving. Fuck. We're not going to get out of here in the truck. Opening the door, I grab my blade from the glovebox and shove it in my boot.

"Come on." Taking her hand, we walk to the back of the club where more people are scattered. A set of double doors are wide open, a staircase leading down into Bare Flesh. It would be easy for anyone being held down there to escape. Kelly was never forced to work here. Leo was either fed lies or conjured them up himself.

"There." Lily jerks her arm to a path cutting through a hedge. Picking up our pace until we're jogging, we take the route, coming out on a sidewalk.

"Dammit," she hisses, checking her foot.

"Take my boots."

"No." She shakes her head and carries on walking barefoot.

"Your feet are going to get shredded."

"Shut up and let's go."

The familiar roaring of motorbikes growls through the night. Headlights beam from further up the road. "Are they coming this way?" Lily freezes. Rumbling seems to vibrate the air we're breathing. Steel and leather come into view, and I grab Lily and race toward a treeline, ducking her behind a huge trunk, the branches obscuring us as the parade of bikes pass. Their patches read clear under the streetlights. "It's my brother," she whispers, squeezing my hand. "Do you think they're going to Flesh?"

It would be an odd coincidence if they weren't. "Doesn't matter. We're not there." Creeping along a row of closed shops, we keep to the shadows. A closed sign flickers in one of the windows lighting Lily's face. "Why are you smiling?" I tease.

"It's been a crazy night." She breathes. I attempt to cross the road, but her hand tugs on mine, pulling us down an alleyway.

"It's a dead end." I shake my head. A frown tugging on my brow.

"I don't care." Pushing me against the wall, she jumps on me, and I catch her on instinct.

"What are you doing?" Her thighs fill my palms, her dress riding up to her waist. My breathing accelerates, and my dick perks up.

"Fuck me, Zane."

"Here?" I don't know why I'm stalling. Every part of my body wants to touch hers, but she has a past. Am I taking advantage?

"Don't think, feel. Who knows what's going to happen to us after tonight. I'm asking you to fuck me." Her tongue sweeps across my lips as she rotates her hips.

Adrenaline courses through my veins, sending all reason out the window.

Turning, I pin her back against the wall, kissing her

hard and rough. She tears at my hair, shirt, skin, feeding on me like a starved animal. Small hands slip into my jeans, tugging the fly open and diving inside to stroke my hard cock. There's no foreplay or niceties. She's in control.

"Tear my panties off," she breathes, stroking up my shaft. Fisting the material, I yank until it snaps, and she lines up her pussy, thrusting down on me without hesitation. Her wet pussy swallows my cock, squeezing. Shit, I almost come from that alone.

"Fuck me with your fat cock, Zane," she pants, wiggling her hips, her lips, teeth, and tongue exploring the skin of my neck. I piston my hips, fucking her, taking everything she offers. Fisting her hair, I suck her neck, bite her jaw, and kiss her lips until we're moaning. Skin slaps skin. The sound of passing cars don't faze her. She's lost to the madness, and it's stunning. "Harder," she cries. I drive my hips deeper, harder, until she calls out, and my cum spills inside her.

"Mmm…" she groans, peppering my face with kisses. "I needed that." Lowering her to her feet, I readjust my clothes still wet from the sprinklers and chuckle, heat flooding my body. The breeze feels good against the sweat coating my skin.

"What now?" she asks, brushing down her dress.

"We need to get Leo."

"We're not far from the church." She grins, her chest rising and falling.

"Tonight?"

"We might not get another chance. Ronaldo is dead. The Aires will want retribution.

"I'll kill them all before I allow them to touch a hair on your head." Anger like a bomb inside me erupts at the thought of anyone hurting her. She's a Royal Bastard. Her brother will go to war for her. No one is coming for her. Me, on the other hand—they'll want blood. This may be our last opportunity, and I want to make that cunt suffer.

"Fuck it. Let's do it."

CHAPTER
EIGHTEEN

LILY.

Standing in the cemetery, my heart ricochets against my chest. Soft grass brushes between my toes as we creep through the dark like ghosts risen from the graves. "There's an open grave," Zane murmurs, moving toward a row of chairs, almost tripping over a wreath laid out next to the hole.

"They must have a funeral tomorrow." That pig has no right to perform anyone's last rites or funerals. How many others has he assaulted? How many more will become his victims if we don't stop him?

It's almost poetic, losing his life in the place he feels safest.

We came in from the back so no one can see us from the street.

A warm orange glow lights up an upstairs room. Sickness churns my stomach. Memories assault me. Phantom pain throbs beneath my skin. The bruises I wore for days...weeks...after his visits...

"On the bed, Lily."

"Lily," Zane whisper-yells. I hadn't realized I'd stopped moving. Tears stream down my cheeks. "I'm coming."

"Are you okay?" He cups my face when I reach him, concern alight in his blue ocean eyes. "You don't have to do this. I can do it alone."

I've known this man all of five minutes, yet something stirs inside me, reaching out toward him, a thread tethering our souls. Dark and damaged but united.

"No, I have to be there. We do it together."

"Okay. You knock on the door. He'll think you're in distress and a nonthreat."

I nod my head in agreement, and he flattens himself against the wall beside the back door, signaling with his eyes for me to knock. Gulping past the lump in my throat, I will my feet to hold steady and rap my knuckles on the window.

My bones rattle. A light flicks on downstairs, and a few seconds later, a black silhouette walks toward the door.

"You fucked with the wrong girl, motherfucker," I grit out as the knob turns.

"Get on the bed, Lily."

The door opens, and he squints his eyes, looking me over. "I know you." His voice washes over me, coating me in ice. He steps toward the threshold, his dark hair swept off his face, his acne scars like burns, making his cheeks ruddy.

Zane moves like a cat, quick, graceful. "Don't know me, motherfucker," he growls, his knife clutched in his fist.

Forcing his way in, Zane braces his forearm against the devil, backing the evil inside the house. I check the surroundings. Greeted with only the dark night, I race inside and close the door.

Zane wrestles with the devil, jabbing him in fast, precise movements.

Pushing away my fear, I edge farther into his lair. He's a big bastard. He fights back, throwing Zane over a couch and tumbling on top of him. Swinging, he connects a fist to Zane's jaw. There's no collar, no power, just a sicko in his sleep pants and a white cotton shirt, blood soaking through it.

The scales have tipped, motherfucker.

Sauntering up to him, energy zipping through my veins, I lift my bare foot and boot him in the face, knocking him off Zane.

Snatching the knife, I taunt, "I remember you too."

"Lily…" he wheezes, holding up one hand, placing the other against his ribs. Stab wounds litter the side of his body, purposeful strikes to puncture the lung and kidney. Zane is a special kind of animal.

My kind.

Standing over the rapist's thighs, I lean over and grasp the fabric of his pants in my hand, yanking them down.

"Stop! Why are you doing this to me?"

"You fucking know why." Zane dives for him. He straddles his chest, pinning his arms to the floor. The devil attempts to buck him off, but he's weak, the wounds already seeping the life from him.

Dropping between his legs, I pinch his flaccid cock between my forefinger and thumb and extend it, swallowing the acid burning my throat. I place the metal blade at the base and begin carving, relishing in his screams, feeding on his fight as he attempts to close his thighs but only traps me between them.

I've never heard a man wail like a child before now. The skin rips. Pink, flesh-like jelly oozes with a shit ton of blood. I store that scream away in my memories to call on when the bad dreams attack.

His disgusting cock comes away in my hand. I get to my feet and walk around Zane, dropping to my knees at the devil's head.

Pale skin and tear-filled eyes stare up at me. "Open," I demand, slamming my palm down on his jaw and shoving his cock into his mouth until it sits in his throat. Covering his lips, I push down, watching him suffocate painfully, cruelly.

Justified.

"If there is a god, I hope he never forgives you. See

you in hell." I smirk as his body jerks one last time then stills.

A chuckle bubbles out of me. Elation courses through every fibre of my being. "We made a mess." I wince.

"We'll put him in the hole out back and cover him with mud. They'll lower the coffin and no one will be the wiser."

"And this place?" I look around. Blood coats everything in sight.

"We clean and hope." He shrugs, wiping his brow with the edge of his shirt, giving me a glimpse of a tattooed torso. "I saw a wheelbarrow in the yard." He gets to his feet. "Check the kitchen for cleaning supplies."

"Zane!" I call, halting his steps. Walking to where he stands, I grasp his cheeks and stand on my tiptoes, caressing his lips with mine. "Thank you," I murmur against his mouth, pulling away. I turn, but he grabs my wrist.

"Whatever comes next, I don't regret a single thing we've done together." His eyes bore into mine.

"Me either." A grin curls my lips, and he releases me.

We may have been Bonnie and Clyde in a former life.

Finding the kitchen, I scan the small space. It's plain, white, baron. Canned food sits on the counter, and that's it. Nothing.

I open the cabinet under the sink. A red bowl, a dish rag, and a bottle of toilet cleaner. Great.

Filling the bowl with hot water, I go through the house. From the front doorframe, down the walls, floors, every piece of furniture, I scrub until my fingers are sore, emptying and refilling a hundred times, until there's not a speck of blood and our fingerprints are erased.

"Lily," Zane calls out from another room. Walking through the hall, I follow the sound of him shuffling things around and enter a small office.

"Did you bury him?" I ask, frowning. Blood and mud cake his clothing, but his pinched features and pale skin make me step away, my back hitting the wall. He's looking through a box—the same ones at my grandparents' house.

No.

"There are hundreds of images, Lil. Fuck this motherfucker." Zane gags, throwing the picture he's holding back in the box.

"Is it me?" I ask, my voice fragile to my own ears.

Whipping his head up, he levels me with a steely gaze. "No. Why do you think he took pictures?" He sweeps through the images, searching. My heart pounds through every inch of my skin.

"Get on the bed, Lily."

No. No. No.

I fucking won.

He's dead.

I'm here.

"I don't see anyone who looks like you. Let's burn the place." He throws the images down on the desk, scrubbing his hands down his face.

"No. Let the police find it. They'll think he skipped town." Feeling returns to my limbs and I grab the box, tipping out the rest of the images onto the desk. Some scatter to the floor. "Everyone will know what he is."

"Are you sure?"

"Yes. Come on. Let's get out of here."

Taking my hand, we double-check the house then leave the way we came.

The cool air bathes my skin. The rising sun kisses the horizon. I breathe easier.

I won.

"Please take my boots," Zane puffs out.

"We're almost there." I wave his hand away.

"Get on my back then," he insists.

I take off running toward Kirby's. The world is waking up, and we both look like characters from a horror show. Heavy footfalls fall in line with me, and I know without looking he's frowning.

My lungs begin to burn. My cheeks heat. Sweat breaks over my skin. I slow to a jog. "We're almost there. Come on," he urges. I groan, picking up my pace. The soles of my feet burn like Satan is lighting a fire beneath them. With our body count tonight, he probably is. My car comes into view, and I sag in relief.

Whipping his tee off, Zane says, "Unlock the doors."

"I didn't lock them." My gaze drops over his blood-stained skin, the ink moving with his actions. Damn, I hope we get to fuck again soon. Naked next time. "The keys are in the car." I wave my hand toward it.

"Lily!" He shakes his head like I'm crazy.

"Where would I have put them?" I spread my arms wide, gesturing down my body.

He rounds the hood and gets in the driver's side, shaking his head again when he pulls the visor down and the keys slip into his hand. Opening the passenger door, I fold into the seat and drop my head against the rest. "I could sleep for a week."

"Let's shower first."

"Together?" I bite my lip.

"You read my mind."

I open the center console and pull out my cell. It lights up with million missed calls and a barrage of texts. "Shit."

"What?" Zane asks, kicking the engine over and pulling out of Kirby's.

"My brother has been blowing up my phone all night."

Bro: Where the hell are you?

Bro: Get home now.

Bro: Answer your damn phone, Lily.

Bro: The whole club is looking for you.

Bro: Monroe is freaking out. At least tell me you're safe.

I flit my fingers over the screen, typing out a text.

All is good. I'm fine. Met someone. Going on a road trip.

The phone rings immediately. "Fuck my life."

Clicking the icon, I answer, my voice saccharine sweet. "Yes?"

"I know who you're with, Lily. Get your ass home now. Tell Zane he has one chance to do the right thing." Jameson's tone is deadly. A zap of apprehension climbs up my spine.

"What's the right thing?"

"To fucking bring you home."

I end the call and tap my hand against my leg, avoiding Zane's glare.

"What did he say?"

A beep alerts me to an incoming text. Opening it up, my stomach twists.

"What is it?"

"The Royal Bastards have Leo." I flash him the picture of Leo sitting on a chair at the clubhouse, weeping, his lip bloody.

"So much for not getting involved." He slams his palm against the steering wheel. "Dammit."

"They know we're together. Maybe that's why they got involved. This is my fault."

"No. This is Leo's fault—and the stupid woman who played him."

"What are we going to do?"

"I'm going to take you home."

This doesn't feel right. If Jameson hurts Zane, I'll never forgive him. "What if we run?" I suggest on a whim. It will be hard leaving Ruby, but I can reach out to her once we settle somewhere.

"They have Leo." Zane shuts me down.

"So? He got you into this mess." Rejection stings.

"Lily, he's my brother."

Static hums in my head. I can't think straight. "Fuckkk!" I roar, frustration coiling my muscles.

"It'll be okay. You'll be okay." He reaches over, rubbing his hand on my thigh.

"And what about you?"

"Doesn't matter."

Fear rears up, staining my heart in black tar. "It matters to me."

Pulling the car over, he reaches for me, and I climb onto his lap, desperate to be close to him. Our mouths crash together, feasting like it's the last time we'll ever taste each other. Tears bleed down my cheeks, and my heart aches.

"It'll be okay," he implores.

Climbing back into the seat, I curl in on myself, just like I would after a visit from the devil. Is life really so cruel to give me a taste of good only to rip it away?

"Promise me?" I whimper.

When he doesn't respond, I die a little inside.

CHAPTER
NINETEEN

ZANE/CHAOS

"This doesn't look good," I groan, pulling into the clubhouse. Rows of bikes, trucks, and cars fill the yard.

Lily fidgets next to me, a solemn presence washing over her. "Let's just turn around."

"They'd never let me take you, Lily. Your brother would hunt me to the ends of the earth."

"It's not taking if I go willingly."

"Be brave," I tell her. Trepidation trickles into my blood about walking into the club. Not for her, though. A calm settles over me, knowing she's safe. We defeated her demons. These last couple of days are enough. If I die tonight, I'll go happy. "You ready?"

"No," she snaps, pushing the door open and climbing out of the car. Without waiting for me, she races to the entrance, yanking the door wide and disappears inside.

Following her path, my heart pounds, adrenaline spiking. Entering the clubhouse, my steps pick up their pace when Lily's high-pitched screeching fills my ears. I round the corner, and silence falls over the room.

There are leather cuts everywhere. Loki from the Reno chapter juts his chin out in greeting, followed by Koyn, Prez of the Tulsa chapter. I've partied with both over the years. Almost a brother myself if I'd just accepted Animal's offer to join. I always knew the road would lead here. Me at their mercy for something Leo got me into. My gaze falls on my brother tied to a fucking chair in the centre of the room.

Jameson flies toward me, his fist reared back.

"Stop it!" Lily screams, smacking his chest, halting his advance. "How dare you!" She jabs a finger in his face. "How fucking dare you!"

"Do you understand the danger he's put you in?" Jameson roars, veins bulging in his neck.

Rage gets between them. He pushes Jameson back toward Animal and drags Lily by her arm to stand beside him.

"You fucked up." Animal clears his throat. "I should have been at home with my wife, waking up with my kid. Instead, we get security footage of you and Lily entering Flesh."

"So? We like to get freaky," Lily calls out.

Animal glares at her, punching a fist toward her.

"Shut the fuck up. You cause nothing but havoc. Thank your lucky stars Jameson is your brother. Otherwise, you'd be out on your ass for this shit."

Jameson bristles, and Rage's jaw ticks.

Turning his fury on me, Animal barks, "Everything you fucking caused tonight was for nothing." He steps up to my brother and slaps him upside the head, and my spine straightens. If he decides to kill him, there's nothing I can do but watch.

"Tell him where this girl is."

Tears fill Leo's eyes. Snot drips from his nose. "Dead."

"He doesn't know what he's talking about. He's been off his meds since she left," I inform them. Animal knows how Leo can get.

"When we went to his house, we found him digging in the yard."

The hairs on my arms lift. I scan Leo's body. There's mud caked all over his knees. "I'm sorry, Zane. My mind kept playing tricks on me." He sniffles.

"He has nightmares," I defend, taking a step toward him, the curse to protect him forcing my hand.

"She was in the hole," Animal informs me, and I stagger backwards. Mom's rantings play back to me.

"Why did you do it?"

"Why did you put her out there?"

Leo's dreams. He fucking killed her.

"I don't remember doing it." He begins to sob.

"Clearly, he's mentally ill. Why do you have him tied to a chair, Animal?"

"Don't fucking question me in my own club! I have him because you went on a rampage with one of our own!" he bellows, spit flying from his mouth. "What happens next is on you! I warned you."

Rage grabs Lily's arm, and she thrashes in his grip. "Don't...please..." she pleads.

"It's okay," I call out to her, my eyes clashing with hers. "I wouldn't change a moment with you."

I accept my fate if it's death. When four brothers surround me and grab my arms, panic seizes my joints. "Wait—what are doing?" I can't move. They're restraining me.

No.

Not Leo.

No. No. No.

Footfalls come from behind me. A man in a navy-blue suit strolls into the room. Awareness crackles through the brothers, a silent respect.

"Do you know who I am?" he asks with a British twang. His eyes find Lily. Tilting his head, he sweeps his gaze over her. Blood and grime soak her dress. Red speckles coat her skin and hair.

She still looks stunning.

"Don't make me ask twice," he warns, dark eyes turning on me.

"Arlo Aire?" I guess. Animal warned me Ronaldo had family. I knew he used his connection to plant fear in people, but I didn't expect them to actually show up for him. He was a dick.

Aire dusts lint from his sleeve then looks at me, a sinister smile taking over his features. Not many men get a rise out of me, but this fucker chills my blood.

Opening his jacket, he pulls something from the inside pocket.

My heart thunders in my chest. I jerk in the brothers' hold, but they don't give an inch. "When I was thirteen, my father gave me this." He flips open a knife. It's a small pocketknife, the type you have as a multitool on a keychain. "He told me when someone wrongs you, they pay with pain so they remember never to cross you again. Pain lasts. It imprints fear."

"Nooo!" I scream, my voice breaking as he stabs the small metal blade into Leo's neck.

My legs give out, and I collapse to the floor, my arms still held above me. Palming Leo's forehead to keep him in place, Aire rips the knife down his artery. Blood spurts out, splashing to the floor.

Leo's eyes expand, and his mouth gapes.

Tears blur my vision. My throat goes raw as I yell out for him.

All I ever wanted was to keep him safe. His gurgling breath rips my heart in two. There's a flash at the corner of my eyes then everything fades to nothing.

CHAPTER
TWENTY

LILY.

"You bastard!" I cry out when Halo clocks Zane with the butt of his pistol, knocking him out cold.

"It was a mercy." Halo rolls his shoulders and cracks his neck, moving away from Zane.

"It wasn't even him. I killed Ronaldo!" I screech.

Rage tightens his hold and growls into my ear. "Shut the hell up."

"And I'd do it again! He was a pig," I add, ignoring Rage's warning.

"Lily," Jameson and Animal bark in unison.

Aire holds a hand up to stop them, a smirk tugging his lips as he studies me. "Let her speak." He towers over me, matching Rage in height but not stature. The suit fits his frame like it was created around his slender form. You can tell when a man takes care of himself. Hair coiffed to perfection. Leo's blood the only blemish on his skin. This man is tailored, expensive, cared for.

A gasp chokes from my lips, and my blood solidifies when he strokes the pad of his finger down my cheek. "Ronaldo's?" he asks, holding up the digit, a smear of blood now coloring the tip.

"No." The corners of my lips curl into a satisfied smile. "But they both bled the same color and cried for their life." I'm antagonizing, but it's the only weapon I have. This man is danger. It oozes off him. We fucked up at Flesh. There's no going back in time to change it.

"What a dilemma you've created," Aire tuts, strolling over to Leo, brushing his shoulders like he's a friend, not the dead guy he butchered.

"The girl is off limits. You can do what you want with Zane," Animal pipes in, Jameson ready to explode.

"No." I pull at Rage's arms restraining me but get nowhere. "Leave him alone. I'll do whatever you want."

"She intrigues me," Aire says, aiming the statement at Jameson.

"You heard Prez," Jameson grunts. Koyn moves from the stall he's sitting on to stand beside Animal.

"The girl is one of us," Loki adds, cutting his gaze to me and winking. It's been a couple years since I've seen him, when we took out Fisher, but he hasn't changed. Still gorgeous and deadly.

There's a shift in the atmosphere. A tense fog builds, infecting everyone. If Aire wants to inflict pain on me, this will be war. I brought this on us. After everything this club has been through, I've been selfish and reckless.

"Why don't we let her choose?" Aire offers, pointing to me as he surveys the room. In two strides, he's back in my face, the scent of power shrouding me. "I'll make you a deal. Give me a year." My gaze snags on the movement of his mouth. "You can pay back your debt by working for me."

"You're not fucking taking her," Jameson growls.

Rage shoves me behind him and juts his chin toward Zane. "Take the boy."

"No, I'll do it!" I call out.

"The fuck you will," Jameson barks, waltzing over to where Aire is standing. "You get Zane. Make him work or kill him, I don't care. It will be over my dead body you take Lily out of here."

"I'd rather it not be," Aires states, not showing an ounce of fear despite being outnumbered. This man is pure confidence, nothing like Ronaldo's arrogance.

"I'll give you a day to decide." Aire pulls a cloth from the pocket of his slacks, wipes the blood from his cheek, then tosses it on Leo's corpse.

"Zane goes free," I call out, winding my body from behind Rage.

"Lily, no," Jameson breathes, grabbing for my wrist. I twist out of his hold.

"You don't get to tell me what I do. I'm an adult. I make my own decisions," I tell him. Turning my attention back to Aire, I state, "No harm comes to Zane, and I'll do it. One year."

"One year." He holds out his hand, and I slip mine into it, ignoring the electricity zapping through my palm. "I'll be back for you in two hours. I think you'll like New York."

I pace my bedroom floor, staring at Zane as Monroe stitches the gash on his head. "Your brother is beside himself, Lily." There's a softness in her voice that comes from being a healer. I'm glad Jameson has her.

"It's a year. He could use the break," I scoff.

"Don't ever say that."

"At least I'm breathing. Aire could have killed me."

"He would have had to go through every brother here."

"Exactly. I'm not being the cause of that."

She dabs around the stitches to clean the tiny dots of blood then throws her equipment back into her bag and gets to her feet. "He's going to have one hell of a headache, but he'll live."

"That's the least of his problems." Seeing Leo murdered…it's going to haunt him. He'll want revenge and be entitled to it.

She pats my shoulder, and I cover her hand with mine.

"One year," I whisper.

The door clicks closed with her exit, and I take up the space beside Zane, resting my head on his chest, absorbing his warmth, counting the soft beats of his heart. Movement shifts beneath me. A groan rumbles up his throat.

"Zane?" I murmur, sitting up.

He blinks his eyes, lines creasing his brow, tugging at the stitches. "Argh…" he hisses, raising his fingers.

"Don't touch it." I drag his hand away and keep hold of it.

"Fuck. Fuck. Fuck. Leo—he killed Leo."

"Shhh…it's okay."

Water wells in his eyes. His chest vibrates. Sitting up, he swings his legs off the bed and snatches his hand from mine, running it through his hair. "I need to bury my brother."

In the next breath, he's on his feet, slamming the door open so hard, it bounces off the wall, knocking a mirror to the floor. Shards of glass splinter like confetti.

"Zane," I call after him, giving chase until we're in the main room, sucking all the oxygen out of it. Brothers still crowd the space, but Leo's body has been moved. There's no evidence he was ever here.

"Where's his body?" Zane shouts.

Animal unfolds himself from the couch toward the back of the room and makes his way toward us, flanked by Rage.

"I fucking warned you what would happen." His anger is like fists.

"Leo didn't deserve that. It should have been me."

"You can thank Lily you aren't with him."

Zane cuts his eyes to me, searching my face.

"I made a deal with Aire." I shrug.

"What kind of deal?"

"A deal where you get to fucking live—but not in my town. You get one day. Sort your shit out. I want you gone," Animal demands.

"Lily?" Zane stresses, ignoring Animal.

"Work—I'm going to work for him."

"Work for him?"

"It's going to be fine."

Animal turns to leave then pauses, looking back. "A word of warning from Aire—you're not welcome in New York either. You show up there, the deal's off."

My stomach twists.

Grasping my cheeks in his palms, Zane lowers his forehead to mine. "Come with me. Let's just go like you wanted."

"I can't. Aire will take it out on the brothers." I wrap my fingers around his forearms and breathe him in, holding onto us for a few seconds more. "One year. I'll come find you in one year," I tell him, a lump expanding in my throat.

"I don't regret a single second with you," he tells me again. "I'll be waiting for you."

Swiping away my tears, I pull back and race to my room. I can't watch him leave.

One year is nothing. Dragging a duffle bag from beneath my bed, I go to my dresser, pull out my clothes and shove them in. Zipping it up, I toss it over my shoulder and give one last look around my room.

Opening the bedroom door, I hit a brick wall of Jameson. "You don't have to do this."

"Yes, I do. Don't make it harder."

"I have something for you." He holds up a leather cut, and my jaw unhinges.

"No fucking way."

"Way. We were going to do it right, throw a big party, but staying true to your road name..." he taps his finger against the patch that reads HAVOC, "plans changed."

Dropping the bag to the floor with a thud, I snatch the cut and put it on, beaming at the feel of it on my back. "You're one of us. If you want to come home at any point, call me. Aire doesn't own you—and he sure as shit doesn't own the Royal Bastards."

"I know. Maybe this will be good for me." I shrug.

Leaning down, he picks up my bag and throws his arm around my shoulder, leading me out. Heat ignites my cheeks when I walk through the club, all the brothers hooting and clapping for their new official sister. "Where's Ezekiel?"

"Ruby is sick, nothing to worry about but I didn't call him. He will be pissed at me, but…"

"It's fine."

Animal stops me before I can make it to the exit, dragging me into his arms. "No one dictates to a Bastard. This is your home. A year or a week, we'll be waiting. We always have your back. I had to be a little tough, for show, you know?"

My chest swells. The lump in my throat prevents me from talking, so I nod and duck out before anyone else can say shit that will make me want to stay.

The orange ball in the sky creates a glare against the sleek back SUV waiting for me. A chauffeur approaches, takes my bag, and opens the car door for me.

Slipping inside, the beige leather seats scream luxury. I get the feeling my life's about to change drastically.

One year is nothing.

I've lived with monsters and survived the devil. Aire will be a cakewalk.

The end for now...

Lily's story will continue in a spin-off series.

It's time to live in the world of the Aires.

COMING NEXT YEAR.

ACKNOWLEDGMENT

Thanks to everyone involved in the Royal Bastards world. It's a fun project to be involved in.

Huge thank you to my readers for wanting Lily's story.

My editor Monica Black, I appreciate you! Couldn't have got this done without you!!! Talk about team work.

Thank you to my PR companies, Give Me Books, & Enticing Book Journey.

Bloggers, reviewers, insta, tiktok and facebook posters! You are the backbone to the book world, I appreciate you. Thank you for reading, reviewing, sharing!

And big thank you to , K Webster for this badass cover, I love you.

ABOUT THE AUTHOR

Ker Dukey is an International bestselling author.

Genres include:

Dark Romance, Psychological Thriller, New Adult Romance, Romantic Suspense, Mafia Romance, MC Romance and more. Ker, has over Forty titles published, held multiple #1 bestseller banners and chart-topping titles with the rights sold to numerous countries, translated in multiple languages, and have been adapted into audiobooks

In addition to being an author, Ker is an annoying wife and a mother of three children + one dog (who thinks he's human.) She has a passion for reading and binge-watching crime documentaries.

Find her on social media, where she loves interacting with her readers

Find out more
www.authorkerdukey.co.uk

Printed in Great Britain
by Amazon